Mardi McConnochie was born in Armidale, New South Wales, and grew up in Adelaide. She has a first class Honours degree from the University of Adelaide, and a PhD in English literature from the University of Sydney. She is also a playwright, and works in television as a scriptwriter and editor. Her first novel, *Coldwater*, was shortlisted for the Commonwealth Writers' Prize (Best First Book, South-East Asia and South Pacific Region) and was translated into four languages. *The Snow Queen* is her second novel.

The Snow Queen

Also by Mardi McConnochie

Coldwater

A NOVEL

MARDI MCCONNOCHIE

flamingo
An imprint of HarperCollins*Publishers*

Flamingo
An imprint of HarperCollins*Publishers*, Australia

First published in Australia in 2003
by HarperCollins*Publishers* Pty Limited
ABN 36 009 913 517
A member of the HarperCollins*Publishers* (Australia) Pty Limited Group
www.harpercollins.com.au

Copyright © Mardi McConnochie 2003

The right of Mardi McConnochie to be identified as the moral rights
author of this work has been asserted by her in accordance with the
Copyright Amendment (Moral Rights) Act 2000 (Cth).

This book is copyright.
Apart from any fair dealing for the purposes of private study, research,
criticism or review, as permitted under the Copyright Act, no part may
be reproduced by any process without written permission.
Inquiries should be addressed to the publishers.

HarperCollins*Publishers*
25 Ryde Road, Pymble, Sydney NSW 2073, Australia
31 View Road, Glenfield, Auckland 10, New Zealand
77–85 Fulham Palace Road, London W6 8JB, United Kingdom
Hazelton Lanes, 55 Avenue Road, Suite 2900, Toronto, Ontario M5R 3L2
and 1995 Markham Road, Scarborough, Ontario M1B 5M8 Canada
10 East 53rd Street, New York NY 10022, USA

National Library of Australia Cataloguing-in-Publication data:

McConnochie, Mardi Jane.
  The snow queen: a novel.
  ISBN 0 7322 7698 5.
  1. Ballet dancers – Fiction.
  2. Man–woman relationships – Fiction.
  I. Title.
A823.4

Cover and internal design by Christa Edmonds, HarperCollins Design Studio
Cover photographs from PhotoLibrary
Author photograph by Gene Ross
Typeset by HarperCollins in 11/18pt Sabon
Printed and bound in Australia by Griffin Press on 80gsm Bulky Book Ivory

6 5 4 3 2 1   03 04 05 06

One

1973

Edward Larwood had not been home (if you could call a place that you had fled twice, cursing and spitting, home) in twenty-five years. As the plane descended over the brown, brown hills, bouncing and hiccuping through the turbulent skies, the flat quarter-acre suburbs rose up to meet him and he looked down on them with a strange queasy sensation which might have been caused by the turbulence, or the lewd pinky-grey sausage they had served him for breakfast, or perhaps by something else altogether. Had it changed at all, he wondered, in twenty-five years? Adelaide, his home town, with its liberal traditions and its lucid grid of right-angled streets, its blistering desert heat, brown stagnant river and fabled churches, its air of Protestant respectability coloured by the occasional whiff of sex crime.

Adelaide, the Athens of the south, and how the locals bridled if you told them it was nothing but a big country town!

Another homecoming — his second. He remembered the first time very well: 1946, a slow boat from England, no prospects, no future. He was thirty-four years old and he hadn't been home in sixteen years, and yet it felt as if he had never been away. His home town had reached out its tentacles and dragged him back, like a giant octopus or some other hideous sea monster which bathed its scales in the flat, cold waters of the Gulf.

But how different it was this time! The return of the native, in all his foreign glory — and how they loved a local boy made good overseas. This time he was the chosen one. This time they couldn't get enough of him. This time he had everything he could wish for: respect, esteem, his own company. This time he would make it work. This time he would be the artist he had always wanted to be.

The plane suddenly dropped ten feet and he clutched the blue TAA armrest convulsively, wondering if he was about to be plastered, luggage and all, in a flaming skidmark across the suburbs. Gazing down from his window seat, he watched as women, unconcerned, pegged up washing, dogs sniffed at back fences, and kids splashed in aquamarine swimming pools, while the plane bunny-hopped overhead, buffeted by a howling wind. How could they live so calmly under the flight path, with landing gear skimming their TV aerials? All it would take was one freak gust and this plane, this very plane, could be gouging a burning path of destruction through their garden beds.

But suddenly the plane cleared the last red-tiled rooftop and bounced to a halt, and it was time to clamber off the plane and

One

walk across the tarmac to the terminal. The wind was a hot screaming northerly, and behind the city the backdrop of hills rose up, already baked brown, tinder-dry, although it was only the beginning of December.

He wasn't sure if there would be anyone to meet him as he strode into the arrivals lounge. All around him family reunions were erupting, all startled cries of joy and the wiping away of tears. He hadn't thought to tell his sister when he was arriving. Somehow he couldn't imagine either of them wiping away tears at the sight of one another, but in spite of himself something in him was stirred by the presence of so much familial emotion, and he felt strangely lonely.

But then he noticed the man in the uniform holding up a sign in honour of 'Mr Edward Larwood' and all his buoyancy returned. A chauffeur. How delicious.

He went over with a spring in his step and announced himself.

'Welcome to Adelaide, Mr Larwood,' the chauffeur said.

'Thank you very much,' Teddy said. 'It's a pleasure to be here.'

LARWOOD TO HEAD BALLET COMPANY

Ballet South today announced the appointment of a new artistic director, the well-known dancer, choreographer, actor and director, Edward Larwood. Ballet South has been given development funding by the state government and will now become the state's first professional ballet company.

'Teddy was the obvious choice for the job,' Ballet South chairman, Robert Buckley, said today. 'He's got the talent, he's got the experience, he's got the international reputation the company needs. The fact that he's also a South Australian is an added bonus.'

Larwood left Australia in 1930 to pursue his career overseas. He found fame in London with the Sadler's Wells Ballet, later branching out into acting, choreography and directing. During a long and brilliant career, he danced with many famous ballerinas, including Margot Fonteyn. Although he retired from dancing in 1952, he has continued to appear as a guest artist with a number of international companies.

Apart from a brief stint after the war, Larwood has not lived in Australia since 1930. 'The time was right to come home,' Larwood said. 'There's a real renaissance taking place. Australian artists are forging their own distinctive voice in every area of the arts, from painting to music to literature. It's time we did the same with ballet.'

Larwood announced he would be seeking out new and innovative choreographers and commissioning an ambitious program of new Australian work. 'The ballets of the traditional repertoire are very important, but unless we look to the future, the art form will die.'

The Advertiser, 27 October 1973, p. 11

Three

How can this be? How can they have appointed him? Do they not know what he does to companies? Or is everyone's memory so short?

John tells me to calm down. He says it is *a poisoned chalice*. He thinks the board has set Teddy up to fail. He says I should know better than most that there is no audience in Australia for bold new works on Australian themes. He says the old ladies and the little girls want to see story ballets, the *Swan Lakes*, the *Nutcrackers*, the *Sleeping Beautys*, the ballets with toe shoes (as he calls them) and fairies and lots of pretty frocks. He says Teddy will fail and his contract won't be renewed and everything will go on as it always has and then will I be satisfied?

'No, I will not,' I say. 'It will take a lot more than that before I am satisfied.'

John throws up his hands. 'How long can you bear a grudge?' he asks.

'Longer than you can possibly imagine. I am Russian. We feel things very deeply and we do not forget, we do not forgive.'

'You're not Russian, you're Australian,' says John, 'and it was all a long time ago.'

'Twenty-five years is no time at all to a Russian,' I tell him. 'Our sense of grievance goes back centuries.'

He laughs. He thinks I'm joking.

Teddy gives interviews on the radio, in the arts page in the newspaper, in the *Women's Weekly*. He talks and talks about Sadler's Wells, and the Royal Ballet, about those second-rate films he did in the 1960s after his knees went and he couldn't dance any more, about Margot Fonteyn, about Anna Pavlova (he saw her dance *once*), his glittering life, la la la, so on and so on. He does not mention me.

John is on various boards: he is on the Art Gallery board, the board of the Opera. He knows our arts-loving Premier. We go to many functions — cocktails, openings, premieres, parties, fund-raisers. The talk everywhere is of *Teddy, Teddy* (as if they know him personally, which they don't). They talk as if his life has been nothing but Royal Gala Performances and tea with Audrey Hepburn, as if he has not set foot on these shores in forty years, *which is not the case*. At first I assume they are being tactful, that they do not wish to bring up that sad topic. And then someone says to me, 'You used to dance, didn't you, Mrs Black? Did you ever cross paths with Teddy?'

It is only then that I realise: they don't know. They don't remember. It has all been forgotten. These are people with an

Three

interest in the arts. (A sort of interest. They are not true afficionados, not in the European fashion; they do not love the arts, there are no balletomanes here as there were in Russia. But they turn up to everything, they put their money where their mouth is. It is something, I suppose. John is like this. He will always give money to a good artistic cause.) But they do not remember the Koslova Ballet, our years of touring. They do not remember that for two years Teddy was my *premier danseur*. That we ran the company together (well, that is a complicated matter, but to an outsider, that is how it looked). That while he was with my company we produced *new and innovative* ballets in an Australian idiom. Yes, for a brief stint after the war we did this. Now, it is as if it never happened. This country has amazing powers of forgetting. Everything, everything, is wiped away and forgotten almost as soon as it happens. Here, everyone is so obsessed with the *new*. This renaissance we are having, now that *it's time*, people are behaving as if there was nothing here before, as if no one had ever written a poem or painted a picture or pointed a camera before. Or made a ballet about a black swan, for that matter.

I don't blame Teddy for not mentioning me. Why would he, after all? It is not such a glittering chapter in his life, I doubt he would want to remind anyone of it.

But the rest of them I cannot forgive. *You used to dance, didn't you, Mrs Black?* As if I was some Tivoli girl, kicking up my heels. That he should be fêted while I am forgotten and overlooked, after all I did, it is not right. Not right at all.

We hold a dinner party for twelve. I have bought a fondue set. I make a cheese fondue and I accompany it with sliced bread, salami, pineapple and *crudités*. My guests are very enthusiastic and the fondue is a great success.

My guests are art lovers — that is, they subscribe to everything — and soon the conversation turns to Ballet South and Teddy. Everyone seems to think it is so *marvellous* that he is coming to save our little ballet company. It makes me so furious I could spit.

Perhaps I have drunk a little too much wine and eaten not quite enough *crudités*. When someone turns to me and says, 'I know you're fond of the ballet, what do you think, Mrs Black?' something snaps in me and I say, 'I think it is a *disgrace*. That man is a conniving, destructive, manipulative *thief* and he should *never* have been given a company of his own. I think the appointment will be a disaster and Ballet South will be in ruins within a year and he will be solely to blame. He has no skills as a choreographer and he doesn't really love the ballet. He is a vain, self-serving con artist and he cares about nothing but himself.'

A dreadful silence falls over the table. Mouths are agape. Melted cheese drips from *crudités* onto earthenware plates. My friends all think I have gone mad.

'The artistic temperament!' John says and laughs, and everyone else chuckles too and starts dipping and dunking in the remains of the fondue.

No one asks me to elaborate. No one asks why I loathe and despise him so much. I realise I have crossed a line and said something it is not acceptable to say. The people at my table know the people who anointed Teddy and they have all reached a consensus: he is *a good thing* and must not be criticised.

❋ ❋ ❋

We are invited to a gala to celebrate Teddy's arrival at Ballet South and bid farewell to Alice McDowell. As I say, we are on many lists and are invited to many things. John gave some money to help establish Ballet South. Now they have money from the state government but they are always looking for philanthropists and so we are invited to the gala.

'I'm not going,' I say.

'Don't be silly,' John soothes, 'of course you're going. You'll enjoy it. Even if it's dreadful you'll have fun picking it to pieces.'

'I do not criticise for *fun*,' I tell John severely. 'I criticise because standards matter. And I refuse to show my face at a

Four

gala of his, as if I approve of it, as if I approve of him, as if I have *forgiven* him.'

'No one knows about all that,' John says. 'They'll just think it's odd if you don't turn up.'

'I don't care what they think. Maybe they have forgotten what Teddy did to me, but I will tell them, I will tell them all.'

'Not at the gala, I hope.' John chortles anxiously. 'That might be a bit embarrassing.'

'I don't care if I embarrass him. He deserves to be embarrassed.'

John is not smiling any more. 'If you go along to that gala and make a scene, the only person who will be embarrassed is me. I will be embarrassed. Not him. Is that what you want?'

Of course it is not what I want. John is a dear man and my husband and I love him. I would never do anything to embarrass him.

'In that case,' I say, 'it is better if I do not go. If anyone asks, I have a headache.'

❋ ❋ ❋

After the gala I have lunch with my friends. They have all met Teddy now and think he is *so* charming, *so* gallant, *so* witty.

'But what about the dancing?' I ask. I do not want to hear about what a lovely man Teddy is. I know how charming he can be. It is, of course, a façade. The reality is quite different.

'The dancing was very poor,' says Elaine comfortingly.

'You can't blame Teddy for that,' says Valerie. 'He inherited the dancers.'

'And the repertoire,' adds Phillipa.

13

'If the dancing wasn't very good then there's only one person to blame,' says Valerie.

She means Alice McDowell, the former director of Ballet South.

'I feel sorry for poor Alice,' I sigh.

The ladies gawp at me in amazement. 'But you can't stand her,' says Valerie.

'You've been gunning for her for years,' says Phillipa.

'I thought she was treated very shabbily,' I say. 'She worked very hard for the cause of ballet in this state.'

'You used to say that if there was any justice she would have been taken down a dark alley and knee-capped long ago,' Valerie says. She is looking at me a trifle suspiciously.

It is true that Alice McDowell is my *bête noire* and I have for years longed to see the back of her. To anyone who is serious about the dance, her choreographic effusions are a torment. But her love for the ballet is real and she has struggled against the odds to keep her company going. She must run a ballet school to make ends meet and her dancers are only semi-professional. They are not of the first rank. (They are not even of the second, or the third.) She is often dismissed by critics for being nothing more than a dancing school teacher with delusions of grandeur. It is said she should stick to teaching little girls, that she should know her place. But I too was once the mistress of a dancing school, and I too did not know my place. I had bigger plans, and I brought them to fruition. Of course, I was a serious dancer with an international reputation, so my situation was quite different. But I can almost feel sorry for her.

Four

'I'll admit,' I say, 'I did not have a great deal of respect for her as an artist. But she did the hardest job of all, which is to make *something out of nothing.* Don't you think it is very cruel and wrong that she should work so hard to found her own company, and then when it is on the very brink of success at last, she is dismissed, like a common housemaid, when it was her own company from the start? Does that seem fair to you? It does not seem fair to me.'

'You're not seriously proposing they should have kept her on, are you?' asks Valerie sceptically.

'No,' I say, 'not a bit of it. I'm just saying I feel for her, that's all.'

The other ladies nod sympathetically.

'She wasn't a bad old stick,' says Elaine.

'It does seem very hard,' agrees Phillipa.

'Out with the old, in with the new,' says Valerie breezily.

❈ ❈ ❈

I decide to write a memoir.

John is not encouraging. 'Darling,' he says, 'it's not that I don't think you can do it, but it's quite a big undertaking.'

'You think my English is not good enough,' I say.

'Your English is excellent,' says John, 'but you're not really a word person, are you?'

'How will I know if I am a word person,' I reply, 'until I try?'

It is true that my English is not always perfect, especially if I get excited, and they say I still have a strong accent (myself, I do not hear it). When I first went to Paris I learnt to speak French, and when I came to Australia and decided to stay I worked very hard to become proficient in English. I have a dictionary which I still consult regularly. I read now, a great deal. I did not read when I was a girl, there was no time. Always there were classes, rehearsals, performances. When I was not doing one of these, I practised, or I slept. There was no time for reading.

But where do I begin? With my birth in St Petersburg? My first day of class? My first performance (still a child, a supernumerary, in a cast of a hundred)? Or do I start with my starring roles, my journey to Paris, the tours, my second life in Australia after the war broke out? What do I put in and leave out? There is more than meets the eye to this memoir business.

Eventually I decide that this is to be the story of my company, since the company was my life. Everything else will follow.

Then you will see. Then you will understand.

Five

MY CHILDHOOD IN PETERSBURG — THE IMPERIAL BALLET SCHOOL —
I LEAVE RUSSIA

St Petersburg

You cannot imagine how cold it was in Petersburg when I was young. The cold would enter your bones and stay there for months. It numbed the brain and bit at your flesh. Petersburg is only a few hundred miles from the Arctic Circle and in winter the temperature can drop to thirty degrees below zero. When the snow is on the ground the whole world seems to turn black and white and blue, as if red and yellow had never existed, and the wide, wide river turns into a great plain of ice, a funnel for the wind sheeting down from the north. Just to be near the river is to feel three steps closer to freezing. In Australia you must always worry about the sun, but in Russia it is the winter you must fear. There, if you go out in the snow without protection, the cold eats away at your skin and steals your fingers and toes, one by one. Once I saw a man who was frozen to death in a snowstorm. The skin had been blasted from his bones, and the flesh that remained was black, as if he had been picked over by crows.

In winter when we went outside to play we were swaddled in so many coats and shawls and hats and mittens you could have rolled us along the ground like barrels. My mother coated my face with goose grease to protect it from the wind. And despite all this it was still cold, so cold. Your head ached, and your ears ached, and your teeth ached. But we would get so bored sitting in our warm stuffy apartment all day, and we loved to play in the snow, and my mother thought it was healthy for children to play outside each day, no matter how bitter, so outside we would go.

When first I came to this place where I live now — this little town that they like to call a city, this town in the desert, Adelaide — it felt like home to me because it reminded me of Petersburg. But how can this be, you ask? How can a place so hot be like a place so cold? How can a place so new, so raw, be like a Russian city? In fact Petersburg is not old, not like Moscow. Petersburg is a rational city, an Enlightenment city. It is the invention of one man, Peter the Great. He decreed that there should be a great Mediterranean city in Russia — yes, his own little Venice, at the edge of the Arctic Circle! In this new city everything was laid out according to a plan: the streets, the buildings, the parks. Other cities grow as if in a forest, new

Five

buildings cropping up on old ones like fungus on fallen logs. Rubbish piles up everywhere. There are ghosts and old troubles festering under the roads and in the cellars. Old plague pits, old cess pits, rubbish and filth. Petersburg was created from nothing, out of thin air. It was new and clean, built on enlightened principles. There were no filthy secrets, no slums, no skeletons in the cupboard, no darkness, no squalor. It builds up in time, of course, the filth, but to begin rationally, beautifully, is better than to build upon layers of muck. London is built upon layers of muck. You know it when you walk those crowded streets. They would have done better to start again somewhere else. I have never cared for London.

Adelaide, too, was built to a plan — Light's Vision! — so square, so forthright. The streets so wide, the parks so regular. Of course, Petersburg was once the heart of a great empire and Adelaide was never more than a provincial centre. In Petersburg there are miles and miles of palaces, all different colours, like sugared almonds. There are no palaces in Adelaide. We should not take these comparisons too far.

Ice-skating

Every winter, when the temperature dropped and the Neva froze, there would be hundreds of people skating on the river — children, courting couples, poor people, rich people. Everyone would throng on the ice, and their cheeks would glow in the cold as they skated round and round. I was not allowed to go ice-skating after I joined the Imperial Ballet School. They were afraid we might break our ankles and not be able to dance, and then all the time and expense of our training would be wasted. But I had always skated on the Neva in winter and I did not like to be told I could not do what I wished. So I slipped out.

It was late in the winter and the ice was old and dark, but I paid no attention. How wonderful it was, after my long confinement in the warm stuffy rooms of the Imperial Ballet School, to feel the air on my face, to race and spin and go as fast as I could across the hissing surface of the ice! I was only ten and did not believe that anything really terrible could happen to me. When the ice cracked beneath me and I fell into the water, the shock was profound. Surely such a thing could not be happening to me. Other people fell through the ice and were drowned — but surely not *me*.

I thrashed about, trying to get a purchase, but only succeeded in smashing the ice so that it bobbed around me in scurfy pieces. There had been no one near me, no one had seen me fall. I was wrapped up in so many layers of clothing I could barely move, even if I had known how to swim. Beneath the surface the tide was flowing fast, and I was sucked down, sucked under the lip of the ice, into water that was greenish-black and cloudy. They say that hell is hot and full of flames, but I think not; I think hell is dark, cold, green, filthy water trapped under a thick skin of ice, full of grit and slime and mud, full of the muck people throw in canals and the bilge that pours out of ships. I remember how strange and green it was, the strange green light down there, and so cold I forgot to breathe. Most children who go under the ice must wait until spring to be found, if they are found at all, but I was lucky. Someone had seen me go through. Men came after me with branches and rails and ropes and broomsticks. They cracked open the carapace of ice and they dragged me out. I wasn't breathing when they laid me out, but I am told I vomited icy water and came back to life as if nothing had happened.

The Snow Queen

'The Snow Queen' is a story about a child whose heart is turned to ice, and who is taken to live in the Snow Queen's palace for all eternity, until he is rescued by his sweetheart, who thaws his frozen heart and takes him home. I did not come across this story until I came to the West, but when I did I was very struck by it. I know just how it feels to have a splinter of ice in your heart that will not melt.

My punishment

I got into dreadful trouble when the school learned what I had done. I had been promised a tiny part in a gala performance before the Tsar, and as punishment this was taken away from me. The part was a non-dancing role as the attendant to an Oriental princess, but the princess was to be danced by my idol, the famous ballerina Mathilde Kschessinskà (a former mistress of the Tsar, although I did not know that then). I had competed with all the other girls in my class for the role. The notables of the company had come to watch us, muttering and talking to each other, staring at us so piercingly that the other girls allowed their nerves to get the better of them. Some started to giggle. Others tried so hard to impress that they tripped over their feet or became as rigid as scarecrows. Only I carried on with naturalness and restraint and so I was given the part.

How bitter it was when my part was taken away from me! It was no good telling me there would be other chances, other solos. They were far off in the future and the gala performance was very soon. It was the *best* part, the *only* part worth having. I was heartbroken. The only small comfort I could find in this very miserable state of affairs was that the role was given to my best friend, Natalya Petrovna Kushkina, who we called Natasha. She was a very pretty dancer, very lively, and everyone said she had the best arms and the most beautiful carriage (by which they meant her posture, the way she held herself, particularly the way she held her head) in our whole class. I was sorry to see anyone else taking my part, but at least Natasha was my friend. There were other girls in the class who were less deserving. I could not have borne it if they had got my part.

Perhaps you accuse me of lacking a sense of proportion, to still remember the disappointment so keenly? After all, it was not a real part, I was very young, it meant nothing. But in a professional ballet school you are *never* too young, and a part is never too small to be noticed. Everything matters, everything accumulates, everything is remembered. Once you have made an impression, even if you are only ten, it will be remembered. You will become worthy of notice, you will become *someone to watch*. Natasha had a charmed life at the school from the very moment that I fell through the ice and she took my place at the gala performance. She was marked out as special, pointed at in the corridor, whispered about. Kschessinska made her a little pet, and Kschessinska's pets were always assured of special treatment (alas, that was the way it worked at the Imperial

Ballet; but this was not a failing of the Imperial Ballet alone, I think). It did not help her in the end, Natasha. But that is another story.

Discipline

Ballet is unique among the art forms, because it is the only one that truly unites body and spirit. You must live it every day or you will cease to be an artist. A poet may go for weeks without writing a poem and still be a poet; a painter may do nothing more than admire a view and he is still a painter. But a dancer who does not dance, every day, to the best of her ability, quickly ceases to be a dancer. Choreographers, composers, actors, painters — these can drive themselves to the brink of dissolution and beyond. I have known poets who claimed they could not begin work until they were blind drunk. But this is not a dancer's way. A dancer must devote her life to the exercise of restraint. Too many dancers ruin themselves through self-indulgence. That was never my way. I loved the discipline, the classroom, the daily round of rehearsal and performance. I have seen too much disorder in my life. In ballet, there was always order.

The Maryinsky

In Russia there were two ballet companies: the Maryinsky, now called Kirov, and the Bolshoi. The Maryinsky was the best. I do not say this because it is where I trained, but because it is true. The Maryinsky school was famous for the perfection of its technique. Dancers of the Bolshoi school lacked the polish of the Maryinsky dancers, and tended to be more emotional in their approach, less perfect, more eccentric and individual. In my view, expressiveness without perfect technique is grotesque, but not everyone agrees with me on this matter.

My papa was a dancer at the Maryinsky. He specialised in mime roles, and although he was never a star, he was a popular man. The ballet was part of the Imperial Court and it was a very good place to work. The pay was good and there were generous pensions for former dancers. The Imperial Ballet was like a family, it looked after its members. When auditions for the Imperial Ballet School were held, preference was given to the children of former dancers, although suitability and merit were also important. I was accepted into the school as a boarder at the age of ten. After that I was only a visitor in my family home.

Young people today are slaves to inclination. They only do something if they *feel like it*. They will not take a job unless it is something they *really feel passionate about*. They behave as if every single choice in life is like taking a lover, as if there must be passion in everything, as if the world is not filled with things one must do whether one likes to or not. When I was young, only the rich could behave like this. For the rest of us, we had to take what we were offered. There were no choices. My papa had been a dancer in the Imperial Ballet, which meant that I too entered the Imperial Ballet. If he had been a servant, I too would have been a servant. If he was a peasant, I too would have been a peasant. If he had been a doctor, I would have been a doctor's daughter and later, probably, a doctor's wife. No one asked me what I felt passionately about. I would do what my

Five

parents had done before me, and I would make the best of it because there was no other choice.

The profession I entered is not the same profession now. Now it is for people who *passionately want to be* ballet dancers, it is a hobby which some people make into a profession. Then it was a trade, like being a plumber. There were many girls in the Imperial Ballet who did not love what they did, but were obliged to carry on anyway, out of duty to their families and because it was a good living. It was respectable and a lucky girl could make a good marriage. There were stars of the Imperial Ballet who had married grand dukes and princes. That still meant something then.

I can still remember my papa's benefit performance. It is one of my earliest memories. I was allowed to stay up late and I had a new dress which rustled when I moved. I thought every man on the stage was Papa, until Papa came on himself, and then I knew him at once. The theatre seemed so huge and so grand, and it seemed unbelievable that there could be so many people in the world who had all turned out to see Papa. I thought he must surely be the most famous dancer there had ever been. I remember them clustering around him afterwards, congratulating him, and some of the ladies wept because he was retiring. I can only remember him smiling that night, but I cannot believe it was a pleasure for him to retire. It is never a pleasure for a dancer to retire.

The Maryinsky is one of the most beautiful theatres in the world. Although it can seat more than a thousand, it is an intimate space. The stalls are a half-circle so small you could almost fit them in the palm of your hand, with rows of little

the Snow Queen

chairs standing on a parquet floor which could have been made for dancing. The horseshoe circles of boxes and galleries, stacked vertically on top of one another, barely seem to rise as high as the top of your head, and the grand boxes on either side of the stage are so close that the occupants could be a part of the action by taking a single step from their seats. The Tsar's box, set squarely in the middle of the grand dress circle, floats like a Fabergé egg just beyond your fingertips, almost close enough to touch. The Maryinsky is gilded and delightful, like a grand duchess's jewel box, lined with velvet and smothered in gold.

Of course, like every theatre, the glamour is mostly an illusion: you can only see it from the front, when you are sitting on one of those gilded chairs in the audience. Backstage everything is workaday: brick walls, painted sets, bare splintery floors, ropes and scaffolding, stagehands smoking cigarettes and dancers with chilblains grumbling. But still it has a magic, a charm. I am from a theatrical family and for me theatres are holy places. To walk into a darkened theatre, to sit in the auditorium and gaze at the stage, even under work lights, is to be in a place where people become more than human, a place where life is lived as it should be lived, at full stretch. Most of life is slack, slow and uninteresting, but when you step into a theatre, everything becomes concentrated. We experience all the drama of life crammed tightly into two or three exquisite hours. We spend the rest of our lives waiting for these few concentrated moments.

I have not set foot inside the Maryinsky since 1917. I don't expect I will ever see it again.

Five

Two kinds of dancer

There were always two kinds of dancer at the Imperial Ballet School: those who loved it and those who hated it. I was one of the kind who loved it; but ballet can be a hard thing to love, as many of us discovered.

I found ballet school a disappointment at first. I thought that at ballet school I would have a wonderful wardrobe of beautiful dresses which I would change several times a day. I thought there would always be a full orchestra accompanying my every move, and that I would be able to leap and twirl about all day as I saw fit. I thought that at ballet school I would dance. In fact, that is the last thing one does at ballet school.

Before you ever get to dance, to leap about, to *express yourself* (there is such an emphasis nowadays on *expressing oneself*), you must learn the basics. The first thing you learn is turn-out. You stand with your heels pressed together and turn your whole leg outward from the hip, until your feet form one single unbroken line, with your toes pointing in opposite directions. This position is, of course, unnatural, but young hips are very flexible and the joints will accept it if they are trained up to it. Once you have mastered turn-out, there are the five positions of the feet. Then the positions of the arms. Learning these is rather like learning to tell the time — each arrangement of the arms has a name, and the name is in French. Then come simple movements, which will one day become the more complex movements one sees upon the stage, but at the beginning they are always broken down into their tiniest components. There is nothing creative about this, nothing expressive, nothing satisfying. But it is necessary. To dance, precision is essential.

Not everyone has the inclination or the patience for a life spent drilling, drilling, perfecting movements so tiny that they seem almost meaningless. Sometimes there is music to make the exercises more pleasant, but often there is nothing but a stick banging on the floor to keep time, the voice of the teacher shouting out instructions and (often) criticism. Sometimes that stick will come whacking down on a hand or a backside or a calf. The studio can be a bruising place, in more ways than one. Dancers do not improve through praise, but through detailed criticism and a continual striving to improve. It takes character to survive such a rigorous daily process of self-examination.

How did I learn to love the ballet? I decided to take the long view. If I wanted to be the one in the beautiful dress at the front of the stage, I must bide my time and do my *battements* and my *port de bras* until I was ready to move on to bigger and better things. And at the Imperial Ballet School, where the graduates were all assured of a place in the company, one knew that one's goal was never very far off. Even as students, the lucky few would find themselves cast as courtiers, goblins, sprites, cupids — non-dancing roles from which we could watch the stars perform. However hateful it might be to have one's calves whacked with a stick in the classroom, nobody could watch Kschessinska dance and then listen to the roars of adulation, see the bouquets come showering down upon the stage, admire the boxes and boxes of jewellery she was sent, without wanting to follow in her footsteps. Kschessinska was a *prima ballerina assoluta*, the highest rank of all, and I could think of nothing

Five

more desirable than to ascend to that exalted status myself. If you want to be as famous as Kschessinska you must work, they told us, and so I worked.

But not everyone felt the same way. My friend Natasha liked to tell me all kinds of things which she claimed Kschessinska had told her. She said Kschessinska never went to class and did whatever she pleased. She said Kschessinska could eat what she liked and no one could say a word to her, even when she got a little fat. (And it was true that Kschessinska did sometimes get a little fat. But she was no less a dancer for it. Dancers were not so thin then, although we were expected to mind what we ate, and we all pined for forbidden food, like cream buns.) Natasha said that Kschessinska was a great artist because she was *simply born that way*. Some people had the seeds of greatness in them from birth; greatness was their birthright and their destiny. Natasha insisted that if you weren't born with the seeds of greatness you could never be truly great.

I agonised over this for a long time. Natasha, it was clear, had the seeds of greatness. But did I? Natasha took to ballet like a duck to water, as if her limbs already knew what to do. Ballet, as I have mentioned, is not a natural activity, but it looked natural on Natasha. She could have been part sylph, so natural did she look when she danced. And she was also very pretty, so that your eye followed her whatever she was doing. I was never as pretty as Natasha and I struggled. I worked, I sweated, I had my calves whacked with a stick. My teachers didn't warm to me like they warmed to Natasha. But I worked hard. I worked harder than anyone else. And gradually my work paid off.

I was lucky in one respect: I had long straight legs, and with work I developed a perfect line. Natasha had beautiful arms and a melting, floating style, but her feet were never strong. Trusting to her natural gifts, Natasha would not work hard. She believed her talent was sufficient. But because of this her footwork never grew strong enough to sustain a role of any technical complexity. Natasha excelled in older ballets, where grace and charm were enough to carry you through, but more demanding roles were beyond her capacity.

Natasha could have been a great ballerina, but she was lazy. Natasha never really loved the ballet. She loved the *idea* of being a ballerina, which was quite a different thing. She never grasped the essential truth that being a ballerina was about art and struggle; it was not about the trappings of success, whatever Kschessinska might have told her.

1917

The course of study at the Imperial Ballet School lasted seven years. If the revolution hadn't intervened, I would have graduated in the spring of 1918 and taken my place in the *corps de ballet* at the Maryinsky. But in 1917 the world of the Imperial Theatres, the old Russia, my Russia, the Russia of the Tsars, was swept away for ever, leaving only chaos in its place.

It is no great tragedy in the larger scheme of things that one little girl never had a chance to dance the *pas de deux* from *La Fille Mal Gardée* at her graduation performance, never had a chance to win the medal, never took her place in the company of the Imperial Ballet. No great tragedy when you think about our soldiers dying with no bullets on the German front, the chaos and the madness that gripped my beautiful city of Petersburg after the revolution, the deaths and the hunger and the bodies in the streets. Just a small, meaningless tragedy, one among many. But added together, all those little personal tragedies make up a tally of suffering which is unbearable to contemplate.

I was not political. I had grown up inside the doll's house of the Imperial Ballet School, I knew nothing about what was going on outside. How could I? Whenever we left the school (and that was rarely) we were taken in a sealed carriage which protected us from the outside world. There was no television and we did not read newspapers. All we knew about was music and dancing, shoes and make-up, wigs, costumes, flowers and jewellery. I knew nothing about the progress of the war, except that there were more and more men on the Nevsky Prospect in pieces — missing a hand, a leg, an eye. We gave benefit concerts for the troops and never thought about our own good fortune, safe at home, all our limbs intact.

How could there be a revolution? The Tsar came to our performances and kissed the hands of the ballerinas. He loved us, and we loved him, passionately and whole-heartedly. I had seen first-hand the evidence of his kindness and good nature, so when the revolution came it was utterly incomprehensible to me. The Tsar — a tyrant? But I knew it was not so! He was a good, kind man who loved his people. I asked my papa to explain it to me and he said the revolutionaries love the Tsar but hate the system he represents. Try and imagine, he said, that the Tsar is just an actor playing the role of the Tsar. You can hate the character and not hate the actor, can't you? But, I said, the Tsar is not an actor. He was born to rule. The man and the role are indivisible.

When you are young you imagine the world will never change. You think life will carry on along its predictable path for ever. I could not imagine a world where ballet was not somewhere at the centre of things, but as the events of 1917 unfolded a different reality intruded. The theatres were closed, the students sent home. Rumours began to spread that the theatre would be burnt down, the opera and the ballet broken up. Ballet had always been a great favourite of the Tsar — was it then reactionary, decadent and corrupt, as the Bolsheviks said? If the ballet was to be abolished, what would become of us? What of the pensions the Tsar had paid to all the former artists of the Imperial Ballet like my papa? Would they be left with nothing? How would we live? What would become of us?

Kschessinska's house was commandeered by revolutionaries. They stole her jewellery and ruined all her beautiful furnishings. It was only through the loyalty of her servants that she managed to escape with her life. I was horrified when I heard she had been forced to flee. She had been greatly loved, and after all, what did a ballerina have to do with politics? But it was well known that she had been a favourite of the Tsar. In 1917, that was enough.

After the Imperial Ballet School was closed I returned to live with my parents. They had grown old in my absence and I found them thin, pale and frightened. Civil war gripped the city. The streets were no longer safe, especially at night, and food was scarce. My brother, who was in the army, had not been heard from in months. Someone said his unit had joined the revolutionaries, but I refused to believe that my brother could have any part in such things. The alternative was too dreadful to contemplate.

Before the revolution my family lived in a modest apartment of six rooms, which was a good size for a small family, but after the revolution we were forced to share it with another family who had many small children. The husband was pleasant enough but the wife was a shrew and the children were hideous. They were noisy and did not wash and they always stank. The whole apartment smelt of nappies. Things would go missing from our room and I knew the children were pilfering, but we could not say anything for fear of being evicted. Although we had never been wealthy, we were seen as bourgeois and so we were suspect. To me this seemed very harsh — had I not given my heart and soul and worked until my joints ached and my feet bled to become the best dancer I could be? Was this not work? But no. An artist of the Imperial Ballet was not a worker. An artist of the Imperial Ballet was a parasite sucking the life blood from the true people of Russia, the real workers. Those same stinking, screaming, stealing Russian workers who lived in my house and fingered my things and watched me all the time for signs of counter-revolutionary impulses. Papa's pension was stopped. As the money we had for food dwindled, he followed the lead of our new room-mates and took to drink.

I leave Russia

At first we did not believe the revolution could last — we were sure that soon the Bolsheviks would be overcome, the Tsar would return and order would be restored. It did not seem possible that the West could stand by and see our country torn to shreds after so many of our young men had died to stop the Germans. Surely, surely these Bolsheviks would not be allowed to succeed? But they were allowed to succeed. As the civil war dragged on and on it became clear to me that there would be no return to the old ways. The Imperial Ballet and the life I had known were dead. As time passed and our situation grew ever more desperate, I realised I had to flee.

Many dancers of the Imperial Ballet had followed Kschessinska to the West. For some, it had become too dangerous to remain in Russia. Others could not bear to stand by and see what was happening to our country. For most, it was simply a matter of survival. When I heard from a classmate that there was a Monsieur Scavelle in Petersburg recruiting young dancers to join a ballet company in Paris, I didn't hesitate. I ran all the way to the Grand Hotel Europe to demand an audition. When at last I was allowed in to see him I was surprised that he didn't want to see me dance, but I put it down to the shining reputation of the Imperial Ballet School. I left his hotel room with a contract and a ticket for the train, dreaming of the brilliant career I was going to have in Paris. When my parents heard the news my papa cried, but my mama took me aside and said, 'Go and don't look back.'

I took her advice. In the autumn of 1918 I left Russia for ever.

Six

'You know you're welcome to stay with us, Teddy,' said Deirdre. 'We've got a spare room, it wouldn't be any trouble.'

'I wouldn't want to put you out,' he said.

'You wouldn't be putting us out, we'd love to have you. We haven't seen you in so long, it'd be quite a treat for us.' Ah, that was Deirdre. Reproachful even when she was trying to be nice.

'If the board's willing to put me up in five-star luxury I'm perfectly happy to let them,' he said.

'I suppose it's more what you're used to,' Deirdre said, her lips pursing tight. 'You with your glamorous lifestyle.'

He had offended her. Given a choice between staying in the middle of town in a large, quiet, comfortable room with air conditioning and room service, he was supposed to prefer sleeping on her lumpy spare bed in the savagely hot, west-facing lean-to, sharing the room with pictures of kittens and the boys' sports trophies, while enduring the boundless silences of Deirdre's disapproving husband Len and the infernal chatter of Deirdre herself. Did she honestly expect him to be interested in the doings of her loutish sons, the relatives he had fled halfway across the world to escape, and weirder still, the neighbours and acquaintances of their mother, who, at a distance of no less than forty years, he was expected to remember? ('You know Mrs Parwill who lived up the road? The one with the knitting? You used to love her jam tarts, remember? You must remember Mrs Parwill!') The torture of those long evenings in front of the black and white TV! The inhuman cruelty of Deirdre's cooking! Was it not enough that he had consented to come to Christmas dinner with the assembled ranks of Larwoods, to gobble dry over-cooked turkey and plum pudding filled with carefully saved sixpences ('I kept them after we went metric') even though the mercury was shooting over the century? No, it was not enough. The cuckoo in the nest, he was a walking, talking affront to the decency of the family, and nothing would ever be enough.

❉ ❉ ❉

Walking through town on the way to lunch, resplendent in a purple Carnaby Street suit with a fat paisley tie, Teddy reflected on how *old* Deirdre looked. Although he knew he didn't look young himself (he had admitted defeat on his hair, which was now radiantly white), he was still lean and fashionable and energetic. Deirdre, at sixty-three, was two years older than he (not that he was admitting it) but she looked old enough to be his mother. Her face, eroded by years of sun, looked like a piece

Six

of driftwood, puckishly decorated with a slash of pink lipstick which bled into the cracks around her mouth. She dressed with dreary decency in shapeless old-lady florals, and rolls of fat bulged under her arms. If it were not for the fact that Deirdre had never been much to look at, you would have to say that she had let herself go. How can she bear it? he wondered. Bad enough that you had to *be* old, but why go out of your way to accentuate the fact?

He was attracting stares. The loud suit, paired with his old head and young body, seemed to aggravate people. Two young men called him a poofter, and he thought, although he wasn't sure, that he heard someone spit at him. He kept his head high as he sauntered rakishly down the street. How strange, he thought, how little things had changed. As a seventeen-year-old dandy he had been ducked in a fountain by a gang of toughs and he found it rather hideously amusing to know that their progeny now walked the streets of Adelaide, censoring and sneering, keeping the city mile safe for the timid, the narrow and the conformist.

My home town, he thought to himself ironically. Why am I here again?

In fact there were several reasons, some better than others. First, of course, they had asked him, and it was nice to feel wanted. But there had been other offers, other approaches, and he had turned them down. Why had he said yes this time? Partly for the sun. It had been a bland, mild, indifferently warm London summer and the thought of another bitter winter had been too much for him: he began to sense how it might feel to be old as he faced the thought of that grey graveyard weather seeping into his bones and sucking at his marrow. He got so low in winter, and this one, he felt sure, would be an unusually horrid one. And there was Cee, too. After months of simmering misery, resentment and boredom, things had finally reached a head and they had agreed to part. Nine years had come to an end, just like that. There had been some phone calls, but it felt over, irrevocably over. You could have saved it, you know, Cee had said, that last time, if you wanted to. But you don't want to, do you? And the truth was, he didn't. It had died slowly, by degrees. All that was left to do was bury the corpse, and they'd done that. But nine years was nine years and there was an ease to life that came with having someone to eat with, or go to the theatre with, or nag about the washing up. Now that there was no one again, it was all too hard — going to the cinema, cooking meals, getting out of bed in the morning. He used to mock those friends of his who moaned about not having families or children because they'd be all alone when they were old. That's why you have friends, he'd said scornfully. But now he was beginning to see the point — not of relatives as such (he thought of Deirdre and Len, and shuddered) — but of being in contact with the next generation. Young people had so much energy and enthusiasm. They hadn't been ground down by life. They weren't embittered. They laughed. The thought of having cheerful young people around him again seemed very appealing, so the offer to take up the reins of a ballet company — all those fresh, fun, ambitious dancers — was exactly what the doctor ordered. Your own personal harem, Cee had said bitterly. It wasn't like that, of course it wasn't like that — he was sixty-one years old and he couldn't really delude himself

Six

he'd make any sort of catch for the gorgeous things that caught his eye. (Oh yes, even now. Some things don't change.) But then that was how he'd met Cee, so you never really knew how things would turn out.

But he'd also found, as he got older, that his thoughts were increasingly turning back to Australia. There had always been bright young things crossing the world to move with the fast crowd in London, Paris, New York. But now it seemed that some of them were not in such a hurry to get away and stay away for ever. They were no longer shedding their accents and their colonial manners and turning their backs on the antipodes. Instead they were talking about the things that were happening back home: new theatre and opera companies, shiny new buildings, new opportunities, a new government for a new age. It seemed, at least from the distant vantage point of London, that there might be real change afoot, that the nation might at last be embarking upon the business of inventing itself, rather than being content with provincial mediocrity. Teddy had little patience for nationalistic fervour, but he was always attracted by the sheen of the new. He had met a writer at a party — so handsome, so fresh-faced and enthusiastic — who told him all about the new prime minister, Whitlam, and the new world of funding for the arts. The boy was on holiday but was returning home soon. He had encouraged Teddy to go back. It's a really exciting time, he'd said, beaming. You won't recognise the place.

Ah, youth. In fact there was a great deal that he recognised. The vigilant yobbos in their blue singlets, on the look out for weirdos and long-hairs. The long deathly Sunday afternoons when the city drowsed. Deirdre and her censorious lips. The men in hats. And those accents — the twangy Sydney announcements at Charles Kingsford Smith airport, the affected plum-tones of the Adelaide matrons — at first he thought he'd walked in on a vast national practical joke. They couldn't be serious, could they? But soon it all started to sound natural, familiar, even comforting, and he realised he must have missed being *home*, just a little.

He turned left and plunged down a side street, realising that the restaurant he was headed for was one street over on the immaculate grid of the city mile. This side street was a canyon between tall buildings, punctuated by the yawning entrances to underground car parks. The blistering desert sunlight did not penetrate here, and there was a strong smell of car exhaust. He realised, with a slight prickle about the neck, that someone had turned the corner right behind him — someone was following him. He could hear the squelch of their rubber-soled shoes — was it one person, or more than one? He could see happy Adelaide shoppers criss-crossing in the sunlight at the end of the street, but here, in this shaded cavern, there was no one walking but himself and the unknown other behind him. The walls were blind, windowless. He was quite alone. He remembered the peculiar terror of Adelaide, the eerie expansiveness of those wide streets with no one on them, like the boulevards of some provincial city of the dead. At night especially it was like the return of the repressed, as the lunatics, the drunkards and the perverts came out to reclaim the streets and parks and wide open spaces. The good burghers and their children did not walk those streets at night. They stayed at

Six

home, or shuttled about the city in their cars with the windows rolled up, as if they were on safari. You did not venture out into those threatening empty spaces unless you were looking for trouble. And if you found it, there would be no one to help you. Like Little Red Riding Hood, if you strayed off the path, you were wolf-meat.

All of this came back to him as he listened to the footsteps behind him. He picked up his pace and moved more briskly towards the intersection. If someone came up from behind and coshed him over the back of the head, would anyone see? People were so good at minding their own business here that he could go plummeting down between the parked cars and be bludgeoned to death and no one would so much as raise their head or call out a cautious 'Um ... excuse me ...' All he had to do was get to the intersection. If he got to the intersection he would be all right. He would be surrounded then, there would be safety in numbers, and it would only be a matter of metres until he was safe in the restaurant. His heart was juddering uncomfortably and he was starting to sweat. How loathsome — he would be stinking all through lunch now. If he ever made it to lunch.

He decided to cross the street. Heart pounding, he ducked out between two parked cars, and felt a sudden agonising jolt of pain. He stumbled, astonished, crying out, and crashed to the bitumen as pain shot up the front of his shin. For a moment he was too stunned to understand what had happened. Had the stalker tripped him? How was that possible? He turned and realised that jutting from the back of the parked car was a heavy metal assembly for pulling a trailer, poised lethally at shin-height. As the initial shock wore off, pain began to ravage him.

'Are you all right?' came a voice.

His gaze travelled up from a pair of rubber-soled shoes, to long skinny legs in flared trousers, a red and blue T-shirt, and a mild bespectacled face framed with shaggy unwashed hair. A university student. Not a mugger, not a maniac. A perfectly harmless student.

'I think I've hurt my leg,' Teddy mumbled.

Drenched with shame, feeling ridiculous, he allowed the student to help him to his feet. Suspicion, he thought to himself. It's the suspicion that drives you mad in this place. Suspicion and fear, so you start jumping at every shadow. No wonder they're all old before their time.

His shin was so badly bruised he could barely walk on it and the university student obligingly supported him to the corner and across the street to the restaurant, where he could see the faces of his lunch companions through the window, already cracking open a bottle of wine. They had not spotted him yet.

'There you go, grandad,' said the student, as he deposited him into the care of the *maître d'*.

Grandad. The final indignity.

Seven

The family have come to lunch today: my step-daughter Gwendolyn, her husband Derek, their daughter Sophie (seven) and their son Simon (five). It is Sophie's birthday and I have organised a special party for her. I have a *Women's Weekly* cookbook that has many beautiful cakes in it and menu suggestions for children's parties. I make a hedgehog out of half an orange, stuck all over with cubed cheese and pineapple skewered on toothpicks. I make mini frankfurters (also on toothpicks), sausage rolls cut into tiny slices, fairy bread, frog-in-the-pond jelly. I also make a very beautiful cake shaped like a ballerina, iced in pink and white, with hundreds and thousands on the tutu. Sophie is awestruck when she sees what I have created but Gwendolyn is not so pleased.

'You didn't have to go to so much trouble,' she says crossly.

'It was no trouble at all,' I say. 'I wanted to do it.'

Gwendolyn is annoyed with me for showing her up. She took Sophie and some of her friends to Pizza Hut for her special treat. How can this be a special treat, to go to a *hut*? A child should have a proper birthday party and if Gwendolyn cannot provide it, then it is up to the grandmother to do so. I cannot really blame Gwendolyn, of course. She has recently gone back to university. She does not have time to ice cakes.

Fortunately the children are hearty eaters and they have no trouble eating all the food (not really good for them, Gwendolyn mutters, all that sugar, they'll be hungry again before long). I do not listen to her complaints. It is Sophie's special day and I only care about pleasing her. Sophie puts away six slices of fairy bread and doesn't eat the crusts. John tells her she should eat them, they will make her hair grow curly. Sophie says she doesn't want curly hair. Little Simon says he ate all his crusts. 'Good boy,' says John heartily.

Sophie is a very promising little girl. She is mad for ballet and has started taking lessons. After the meal is finished and the rest of the ballerina cake has been packed away to take home we bring out Sophie's presents. We have bought her a book (*Ballet Shoes* by Noel Streatfeild, a classic), a little pink necklace, and a beautiful tutu which I had specially made. It is pink (Sophie's favourite colour) with a bodice of satin decorated with hearts and roses picked out in sequins. It is very romantic. Sophie is so delighted when she sees it that she runs off immediately to try it on.

'That costume must have cost a lot of money,' Gwendolyn says as we are waiting.

'I don't care about that,' I say. 'I only have one granddaughter, why should I not spend money on her?'

Seven

'She will outgrow it in a year,' Gwendolyn says.

'Then I will buy her another one next year,' I say.

'This ballet thing,' Gwendolyn says, 'you realise it may just be a passing fad?'

'Oh no,' I say, 'I do not think so. She is very young but I think she has talent. I have an eye for these things.'

Sophie comes back then, in the dress. She is dark, like me, and the pink colour suits her very well. It fits her beautifully. She is slender and small, with a dancer's frame.

'Why don't you show us what you have learnt at ballet school?' I suggest.

Sophie becomes very serious for a moment and shows me the five positions and demonstrates a *plié* and explains to me that ballet is very difficult because all the words are in French. But then she loses interest and starts running around looking for some music to put on so she can dance. John puts on an LP of selections from *Swan Lake* and Sophie orders us to sit down and watch while she performs for us. Of course, she has only been taking lessons for a few months, so she knows nothing; but there is a natural charm, a vitality and exuberance there which I'm sure could become true artistry one day, if properly nurtured and developed.

John loses interest first and excuses himself to go and start the washing up. In fact I know he has gone to listen to the cricket on the radio. Derek offers to help. No doubt he has watched these performances before. Sophie dances on, with her little brother Simon bouncing around at her heels, and the concert, I believe, could have gone on for half the afternoon if Simon had not tripped over and bumped his head on the coffee table.

'Enough dancing for now,' Gwendolyn says, as she rushes over to nurse Simon and kiss his head better.

'But, Mummy, I'm not finished,' Sophie says.

'Why don't you go and take your costume off now?' Gwendolyn says. 'We wouldn't want it to get dirty, would we?'

Sophie doesn't want to take the dress off, but eventually Gwendolyn's will prevails and she goes off reluctantly to the spare room to change.

'Who is she studying with?' I ask while Sophie is gone.

'She's just going to the local ballet school on Saturday mornings,' Gwendolyn says. 'It's where all her friends go.'

'What is the quality of the teaching like?' I ask.

'I'm sure it's fine,' says Gwendolyn.

'But what method do they use? RAD or Cecchetti?'

'Method?'

'It is very important,' I explain to Gwendolyn, 'that she should be taught properly. I have seen all kinds of bad habits instilled in children who have been badly taught.'

'She's just having fun,' Gwendolyn says lamely. 'She's only little.'

'I was only little when I entered the Imperial Ballet School,' I say severely.

'That was different,' says Gwendolyn.

'How?' I reply.

'You were training to be a professional dancer,' Gwendolyn says. 'This is just a hobby for Sophie.'

'If a thing is worth doing it is worth doing well. I will find her a proper teacher.'

'You don't have to do that,' Gwendolyn says.

Seven

'Sophie must be encouraged,' I say. 'She must not be allowed to waste her talent in some second-rate suburban dance academy.'

'The local school will do just fine,' Gwendolyn says. 'We don't have the time to be driving her all over town.'

'We will drive her,' I say. 'We don't mind.'

'I think Dad might mind,' Gwendolyn says. 'Really, Galina, it's fine. She's happy where she is.'

I discuss Sophie's training with John after the family have gone home. I tell him I can't understand why Gwendolyn will not take my advice and find her a proper teacher. He tells me I shouldn't take it so personally. I tell him I do not take it personally but I think Gwendolyn is making a serious mistake and that Sophie may not thank her for it later. I tell him I'm only thinking of Sophie's future. John says that Gwendolyn has a lot of ideas she's picked up from her studies at university. He says she thinks it's important to nurture a child's creativity, that it's wrong to force them into rigid rules-based learning environments early in life. I ask him what this has to do with ballet. He says Gwendolyn just wants Sophie to have fun with it, she doesn't want to spoil it by turning it into hard work. I tell him this is nonsense, that it is putting the cart before the horse. Ballet cannot exist without technique, I explain, you cannot simply get up and dance. You must train, you must *work* before you can begin to think about artistry. Ballet can be deeply satisfying but it is not something you do for fun.

'They're her kids,' John says, in that end-of-discussion tone he has. 'We can't tell her how to bring them up.'

I do not understand Gwendolyn's opposition to having Sophie properly trained. Many, many girls take up dancing at

Sophie's age, as Gwendolyn did herself. If it really is so vastly destructive to the young women of Australia, we would surely have seen some sign of it by now.

But as John says, they're her kids and we cannot interfere. Even when it's obvious she's wrong.

Eight

I ENCOUNTER AN OLD FRIEND — STUDY WITH MADAME SEMTSOVA — THE BALLETS RUSSES

Paris

In the years before the Ballets Russes came to the West, dancers were considered little better than prostitutes. Ballet girls were like a harem for rich arts patrons, particularly in Paris. Only men went to the ballet and they did not go to admire the dancing, no; they went to select one of the pretty girls from the display. There was little in the way of artistry or technique, beautiful choreography or costumes. There were just girls in a state of undress.

It was never this way in Russia. In Russia, dancers were always respected.

The Ballets Russes made their debut in Paris in 1909 and

caused a sensation. After that, no one could confuse dancers with whores. Pavlova was not a whore. Karsavina was not a whore. By 1919 no one thought a dancer was a whore, but with so much competition there were many whores who said they were dancers and no one was any the wiser.

By the time I reached Paris, the Armistice had been declared and all of Europe was mad with excitement. Before I left Petersburg I had been told that if you could only get out of Russia there were jobs aplenty for a trained dancer. In London and Paris there were ballets and revues, burlesques, vaudeville shows. They could not get enough dancers, it was said, and Russian dancers were the most highly prized of all. So I arrived in Paris with the highest hopes. I would be dancing Odette on the stage of the Paris Opera in no time!

I soon discovered that Monsieur Scavelle had not been straightforward with me. He had promised he would make me a ballerina in a great opera house and pay me lots of money. When he named the amount it had sounded like a fortune. When I reached Paris I discovered it was not a fortune, it was a pittance, and I was not joining a ballet company. In fact I had agreed to join a chorus line. It was a bitter disappointment to find myself kicking my legs like a common tart, but what was I to do? I knew no one in Paris. I had no friends, no money, and I spoke only Russian. So I took the job in the chorus line, I wore spangles and I did high kicks. What choice did I have?

Natasha

After I had been in the chorus line for three months I had a stroke of great good fortune. The nightclub I worked for signed up a beautiful new star. Imagine my surprise when she appeared at her first rehearsal: a gorgeous, svelte young gamine in diamonds and furs, with coal-black Russian eyes and the reddest rosebud mouth you've ever seen. It was my own dear friend Natasha!

She had been living in Paris for more than a year and had become just like a native. She swore (that first morning, after we had embraced and cried, making everyone at the rehearsal wait) that she had not given up on ballet but was making the best of things performing in nightclubs while she waited for something better to come along. I never did see Natasha make the slightest effort to find a real job in a ballet company, but at that stage she was still taking classes like a serious dancer. It was Natasha who opened the doors of Paris to me. She taught me to speak French (there were many Russians in Paris then, but still it was not easy if you did not speak French) and introduced me to Madame Semtsova, who was the best ballet teacher in Paris. She showed me where to buy stockings, where to get my hats and shoes, how to buy food, where Russian specialities could be found. She showed me how to dress like a Parisienne, and she rescued me from the lodgings I had found, which were dark, damp and very expensive. I don't know how I would have survived those early years in Paris without Natasha. I will always be grateful to her for that.

Madame Semtsova

Every dancer in Paris wanted to study with Madame Semtsova. Some of Diaghilev's girls went to class there, and the girls from the Paris Opera. Her school was known as a place to find the best young dancers. If ever an impresario or a ballet master needed dancers for a company or a tour, he would call upon Madame Semtsova first. This is one reason why her classes were so popular and so hard to get into. I don't know how she managed it, but Natasha somehow found me a place in her class.

There were two kinds of girls at Madame Semtsova's. Russians, like me, who had come to Paris hoping to get a lucky break, along with a smattering of Europeans — Danes, Italians, Poles — who were talented but penniless. Then there were the rich women. Most were Americans, although some were Europeans. There was one, a Swiss, who was very tall and blonde and elegant, like a prize-winning heifer. How I envied them, these girls with their trust funds, or their rich indulgent husbands. Ballet was just a fad for them, but while the fad lasted they came to class every day in their silk tights and their beautiful tunics — a different colour every day, all the colours of the rainbow — and did their exercises like proper dancers. I despised them — amateurs! — but even at the time I knew that they were necessary. Madame took on many dancers who had talent but no money; the rich women's fees subsidised the rest of us. But all the same, I resented them. They would bring their husbands and their loud-mouthed friends to watch us practise. These people would talk incessantly, but they could not be made to shut up otherwise their lovely money might fly away to another studio. Madame had a drunken husband, a count or a duke (they were all counts and dukes then), and her earnings subsidised his drinking, his gambling, his mistresses. She could not afford to frighten away the rich women with their fat wallets and their taste for ballet. Hers was not the only studio in town, although it was the most prestigious. But the facilities were dreadful. The

Eight

studio was on the seventh floor, under the roof. There was no elevator, so it was a long trudge up those seven floors to reach the studio. You were exhausted before you even arrived, and going down after class was even worse. One girl was so exhausted she fell down two flights and nearly broke her neck, but she was back the next day. Both her eyes were black from the fall.

There was a skylight in the ceiling so there was always plenty of light. But in summer, the sun would beat down through this skylight, so that the room got hotter and hotter. Madame took private classes all day, and every hour, every new girl would add her heat and her sweat to the room, until by six o'clock the floor was swimming and the *barre* felt like glue. All those sticky hands — ugh! But in winter it was worse — then it was icy. There was a little stove in the changing room but it was worse than useless, its feeble heat just made the cold studio seem colder. And when the snow fell you thought you were going to freeze to death. 'Dance faster!' Madame would say. 'Warm yourself that way!' I don't know which was worse, the heat or the cold. At the Imperial Ballet School, we were never cold. Like racehorses, we were cosseted and kept warm. They would not let us injure our muscles through working in the cold. So we grew like hot-house flowers.

Gold-digging

For me, dancing to jazz music in a nightclub was like being in limbo. All I had ever wanted was a career like Kschessinska's. There were no compromises for her, no dancing in music halls. A return to the world of ballet was what I longed for. But for Natasha, the life of the nightclub was a dream come true.

Dancing, she said, was her ticket out of Russia, nothing more. Paris, she said, was where she had always wanted to be. (Paris was the centre of everything in those days. Now, I suppose, it is London, or New York, but then the whole world wanted to be in Paris.) Natasha was in one singular way very like the communists: she liked to rewrite history to suit herself. She chose to forget that when she was a girl she had wanted nothing more than to be a great ballerina, that she had believed she was born with the *seeds of greatness* in her. In Paris she laughed at such a notion. She told me I should grow up. Natasha had one goal, and that was to find herself the richest, handsomest man she could get, and the minute she had his ring on her finger she was never going to take another dance class for as long as she lived.

They say Paris in the twenties was one long party which never stopped — only the faces changed. It did not seem so to me. I danced in my chorus line at night and during the day I went to class, in the heat and the dust, the sleet, the snow. After I had paid for my classes and my shoes and my tights and the laundering of my dancing tunics and my tiny room, I had barely enough money to feed myself. I lived on dancing and bided my time. I did not meet anyone and I was never invited to parties. I was not glamorous, I did not know how to have fun. Some women know how to turn poverty into an asset, but I never knew how to make people give me evening gowns and buy me champagne. I had not the knack for it, but Natasha did.

Natasha was a gold-digger and she was quite unashamed about it. I thought that if you were going to behave that way, at least you should be discreet. Not Natasha. She wanted the biggest fattest fortune she could find and she wouldn't settle

Eight

for anything less. No one seemed to care. Natasha was very beautiful, and in some circles that excuses almost everything. Every night men would come for her after the show and take her out and give her jewellery. Natasha pitied me and would try to pass the ugly ones on to me, but I wasn't interested. I did not like American men and I could not understand what they said to me since they spoke only English and I spoke only Russian and a little French. When they offered to take me out for a late supper, I would tell them I was tired and had to get up early the next day to go to class. So eventually Natasha gave up on me.

I suppose it was inevitable that we would fall out. I could not respect someone who squandered her talent for such vulgar and mercenary reasons. (Of course, I knew full well that she had begun to squander her talent much earlier, when she failed to conquer her intrinsic laziness and began to coast on her charm.) I thought it was undignified for an artist to sell herself to a rich man — a nice and young and handsome man, but nonetheless *very rich*. I could not see how she could lower herself, did she have no pride? At first she laughed off my criticism, calling me Miss Prim and 'my conscience', but gradually she became more and more annoyed. 'What happens to you when you are old and cannot dance any more?' she asked me angrily. 'Will you end up taking classes like Madame? How proud will you be when you live in a dusty room and can't afford to eat and must flatter the rich for every centime you can scrape together? What price your artistry then?' But I had no time for such arguments and so our friendship came to an end.

She found a man eventually. He'd done very well out of the war, but Natasha was unlucky. He lost everything in the crash of '29. Still, she had eight or nine years of the high life before it all went bust.

Diaghilev

One day I arrived at class and found Madame talking to a very distinctive-looking man: tall and rotund, with very black hair with a white stripe in it, like a handsome skunk. He had a very haughty manner and I was amazed to see Madame Semtsova talking to him in a shy and deferential manner, like a schoolgirl — Madame who was usually so proud and aloof herself! Although I had never seen him before, I knew him at once. It was Diaghilev! He was looking for a new dancer for his company, and we all hoped we would be the one to be chosen. It was like being back at the Imperial Ballet School, with everyone striving to be chosen for the solo.

Madame set an allegro which suited me very well. I was a strong dancer and was noted for my jumps. We performed this variation in groups of four, trying all the time to see who had caught the great man's eye. Had he noticed me? Or was he watching Nina the pretty blonde, or Lydia in her vivid jewel-coloured tunics? But he gave no sign, watching all of us impassively.

Madame set an adagio. Again, we performed the variation in groups of four. This time — disaster! My foot skidded on a slippery patch on the floor and I was so busy recovering myself that I missed the arabesque. My one chance to show off my magnificent extension — lost! When all the groups had moved

Eight

forward, Diaghilev spoke to Madame. We all waited, breathless with anticipation, as Madame swung round to look at us.

'Charmian, the adagio again,' she said.

Every other girl in the room sighed, as sprightly little Charmian stepped forward and performed the adagio a second time. My heart went crashing to the floor as I watched her tiny little feet and hands, her elfin face. Charmian was a little, quick, pretty dancer of great charm — naturally he would want her. When she had finished the variation, she stepped back and waited.

'That will be all for today, *mademoiselles*,' said Madame.

We all performed a *révérence* and trailed reluctantly back to the changing room. A few of the girls clustered around Charmian and started to congratulate her, but Charmian was having none of it.

'We don't know if he wants any of us yet,' she said.

And she was right to be cautious, for after a moment Madame appeared, and to my very great astonishment looked straight at me. 'Galina Petrovna,' she said, 'may I see you, please?' I had one shoe on and one shoe off but I followed her immediately.

'Galina Petrovna Koslova,' she said, 'this is Sergei Pavlovich Diaghilev.'

I curtseyed deeply. It seemed the right thing to do.

'I am shortly to be mounting a production of *The Sleeping Princess* in London,' Sergei Pavlovich said, in his soft, rounded, rumbling voice. 'If you are willing, I would like you to join us.'

'Thank you, maestro,' I said. 'Thank you!'

And that is how I came to be a part of Diaghilev's Ballets Russes.

Diaghilev's Ballets Russes

As a student of the Imperial Ballet School I was of course familiar with hot-house environments, but never in my life had I experienced anything like the Ballets Russes. To enter the company was to enter a world set apart from reality. The people there were not like people elsewhere: the passions were grander, the enthusiasms wilder, the hatreds more implacable; all of us were united in our love of ballet and of Diaghilev, our incessant desire to prove ourselves and to rise as far and fast as we could, and our disdain for anyone who did not appreciate the splendour and magnificence of our endeavours. I had been in Paris for some time; I had become used to being an alien, a stranger, a little out of step with everyone else. Joining the Ballets Russes was like coming home. The company was like a little piece of Russia preserved in amber, the Russia I had known before revolution and war ruined it, where everyone was lavish and thrilling and larger than life, where everyone was beautiful and art was everything. It was like awakening from a long, long dream — or perhaps falling back into one.

The achievements of Diaghilev and his company are not as well known today as they should be, or as they once were, so I will endeavour to explain what it was that made Diaghilev different. There were many ballet companies touring Europe at that time, most of them led by or featuring Russians. But none of them had Diaghilev's lofty artistic goals. People tend to think of him now as a producer of ballets, but he was so much more than that. He was a total artist without being an artist himself. He knew a huge amount about the history of art and music,

Eight

and he loved opera as much as ballet. He believed that the Russian ballet of the *fin de siècle* (the ballet I had grown up with, and loved so much) was artistically moribund. The quality of the dancing was incomparable, but the music, the design and the choreography were old-fashioned, stale and tired, the work of hacks, not artists. Diaghilev changed all that.

He had an insatiable appetite for new talent. Bakst was an early collaborator, along with Matisse, de Chirico, Picasso, Cocteau, Chanel, Stravinsky, Prokofiev, Satie, Ravel, Debussy. Under Diaghilev's intense and expert guidance, these great artists worked to produce a new kind of theatrical experience, a ballet in which all the elements — art, music, choreography, dancing — were equal and essential. Diaghilev questioned everything: must a ballet have three acts, a story, a star and a corps de ballet, a beautiful score, set and costumes? What was essential, what was inessential? Could a ballet be a single act, or no more than a *pas de deux*? Did it need a ballerina, or a set? Must it be danced to a classical score, and did that score need beautiful melodies, or could it be jazz or ragtime, or the strange angular spikes of modern music? Could a dancer appear in bare feet, or a simple tunic, or street clothes? Did it even need a story, or could a ballet be about a mood, or an idea, or a colour? If the dancers did not turn out their feet or point their toes, if the whole idiom of the movement was new and invented and alien, was it still ballet?

But Diaghilev was not simply interested in the new. When I joined the company in 1921, I was hired to join Diaghilev's production of *The Sleeping Princess*. This was no new and modern interpretation, oh no! It was Marius Petipa's own

Sleeping Beauty, with music by Tchaikovsky, which had been in the repertoire of the Imperial Theatres for many years and was a favourite of Russian audiences (although quite unknown in the West), in a sumptuous (and very expensive) production with all-new costumes and décor by Bakst. The costumes were hugely elaborate and very heavy and difficult to dance in, but the effect was so ravishing that we didn't mind. It surpassed anything that the Imperial Theatres had done in terms of artistic standards and sheer splendour, and Diaghilev hoped that it might run for months or even years like the musical comedies which were starting to appear at that time on the London stage. The idea was that *The Sleeping Princess* would make the money which would fund the company's more experimental work. Alas, it was not to be.

There were many theories as to why *The Sleeping Princess* failed: the first night was plagued by technical difficulties and was poorly reviewed by an influential critic; audiences had grown used to bold modernist fare from Diaghilev and were not willing to accept a fairy tale ballet in the older style. To the London audiences it seemed hopelessly old-fashioned. We often wondered what would have happened if the ballet had opened in Paris instead of London; but we will never know. What the saga of *The Sleeping Princess* showed was that however much he was interested in the new, Diaghilev still had one foot in the past. The glory of academic technique and the classical repertoire were the rock upon which we built our castle. After *The Sleeping Princess* there were no more forays into the past. Diaghilev looked only forward. But I, for one, was sorry for it.

Nine

Although the doctor had advised him to stay off his feet (his leg had been badly bruised) Teddy was desperately curious to see what he had taken on, so when the offer came to sit in on a company rehearsal he eagerly accepted. What would they be like, his new troupe? He told himself he had no expectations, but in fact his hopes were high. Yes, they were a small company, semi-professional, but then hadn't most companies started out that way? 'Semi-professional' described their cash flow, not their abilities. He knew he could not expect too much, but they must at least be a good provincial company. They'd just secured government funding, after all.

As the cab right-angled its way into the suburbs, down residential streets which grew ever quieter and more narrow, he turned to the driver.

'Are you sure this is the right way?'

'Pretty sure, yairs.'

Frowning, Teddy fell silent.

Eventually they drew up outside an ordinary suburban bungalow. The lawn needed mowing and the woodwork was peeling. Anchored in the couch grass was a sign which read:

Alice McDowell's Academy of Dance
Home of the South Australian Ballet

'Here it is,' said the taxi driver.

He didn't even want to get out of the cab.

❉ ❉ ❉

He was met by a representative of the Ballet South board, who was clearly in a nervous dither. 'It's a pleasure and an honour to meet you, Mr Larwood,' she said.

He wondered if she was about to curtsey.

'Please, call me Teddy,' he said.

'The dancers aren't here yet,' said the woman, who introduced herself as Mrs Sullivan. 'I thought it might be nice for you and Alice to have a chance to chat first.'

'Lovely.'

This was always going to be the tough part — meeting the woman the board had just beheaded.

'We're looking at new premises at the moment,' Mrs Sullivan stammered as she led him inside. 'Now we've got the funding we can afford to move somewhere a bit bigger.'

'I don't suppose Miss McDowell wants the company on her turf any more,' he remarked.

Nine

'Mm, well, no,' Mrs Sullivan murmured, blushing. They walked up the hallway. 'Knock knock!'

She led him into the studio, a large room with a sprung floor, windows alternating with mirrors, ringed by a *barre*. As he walked in he was transported back to another ballet studio, another room filled with mirrors. The year after the war ended. He was broke, desperate, living with his parents (God, the humiliation!). He had walked into Galina's classroom, wrapped in the last tatters of his dignity, and demanded a job. He had been lucky: arrogance always played with Russians. He remembered how vivid she had seemed, like a creature from another world, in her black practice clothes, a jewel-coloured scarf tied around her head, her adamantine features dominated by kohl-rimmed eyes. There was always something splendid about Galina; she gave off the scent of grander days. It never seemed to occur to her that she was just an émigrée ballet mistress.

Alice McDowell rose to greet him and all thoughts of Galina quickly faded. She looked more headmistress than ballet mistress in her suit and sensible laced shoes, but she came forward to shake his hand with all the dignity of a conquered queen.

'I'm very pleased to meet you, Mr Larwood,' she said. 'I've heard a lot about you.'

He wished he'd thought a little more about what he was going to say to her.

'The dancers will be along shortly. They're all very excited about meeting you.'

It was clear that she loathed him on sight. He couldn't blame her really — after all, he had stolen her job — but he knew her type. He had grown up amongst women like this. She would have hated him anyway.

'I know this is awkward for both of us,' he said, 'but I hope we'll be able to work together. I'm sure there's a lot you'll be able to help me with.'

Her jaw clenched like a fist.

'It's nice of you to say so, Mr Larwood,' she said, 'but I think we both know there's not going to be room for the two of us. This is your company now. The board have appointed you and there's nothing more to be said.'

She could not quite disguise the quaver in her voice.

'I think you'll find the company's in pretty good shape,' she continued gamely. 'There's a lot of talent there. I haven't had the money to do everything I wanted to do, but I've got some lovely dancers.'

'I can't wait to see them in action,' Teddy said.

'They're all very eager to know what you've got planned. Whether you'll be keeping them or hiring new people.'

She looked at him challengingly, daring him to insult her precious brood.

'I haven't made up my mind yet,' he said. 'I'll wait until I've seen them.'

❋ ❋ ❋

Well, they could dance, a bit. But they were not a real ballet company, not by any stretch of the imagination. Two-thirds of the company were girls, and an ill-assorted selection they were: some short, some tall, some alarmingly buxom. They were not without talent, he had to give them that, but their ensemble

Nine

work was so ragged they looked as if they had been rehearsing in separate rooms and had seen each other for the first time that day. Where had she found them, he wondered. Were these kids really the best the town had to offer? One of the boys showed real promise, and he could do something with some of the girls, but as for the rest of them ...

He looked over at Alice as the dancers went through their paces. She sat with her back ramrod straight, her face drawn tight by intense emotion. Although her expression was hawkish and stern, it was obvious that she loved her dancers with the fierce ardent love of a devoted parent. He knew now where she had found her dancers: she had trained them all up from babyhood.

When the rehearsal was over they clustered shyly round him and he felt churlish for having been so dismayed. Technically they were a mess, but they were gorgeous kids, so young and so hopeful. He could still remember how it felt to be that age, holding your potential in both hands, waiting to see what the world would deal out to you. Throwing yourself into the icy water, not knowing whether you'd come up swimming or sink like a stone. When it felt like the world was full of people who knew more than you, people with immense power and prestige, people who could make or break you. At seventeen he had marched into Pavlova's class (her last Australian tour, it was 1929) and insisted on showing her what he could do. His repertoire included tap, singing, and recitations from Shakespeare (not to mention his splendid rendition of 'Don't Bring Lulu' on ukulele), but on this occasion he had limited himself to ballet, which he had studied for a little less than three years. The gall of it was breathtaking, but Pavlova had taken it in her stride. The great ballerina had been presented with hundreds and thousands of dancing tiny tots over the years, and she had received them all with a gracious smile before sailing majestically on to her next engagement. To the seventeen-year-old Teddy she had said, 'Charming. If you come to London, you must come and see me again.' He had been hoping for more (Bless you, my child! You are a genius! You must join my company at once and be my partner!) but as he changed disconsolately into his outdoor clothes one of the company members took him aside and said, 'You should consider yourself lucky. That's high praise from Madame.' It was all the encouragement he needed, and within a year he was on the boat to England. What with one thing and another he never did manage to see Pavlova again, but by that time it no longer mattered. Her words — taken to heart, mulled over, treasured — had come to seem like a message from the gods. She had chosen him, singled him out for praise. He felt magical. Special. *Gilded*.

Alice McDowell watched him with quivering disapproval as she introduced him to each one of her charges, as if she didn't trust him to recognise each dancer's special qualities. And of course he *could* see what she saw in them; they all had something. But for most of them, it wasn't going to be enough.

'Lovely to meet you all,' he said as he took his leave of them. Don't give up your day jobs, he thought.

❅ ❅ ❅

Nine

Although it had only been a bad bruise, his leg stubbornly refused to heal and so he was forced to appear at Alice McDowell's farewell gala leaning on a walking stick like some red-faced buffer with gout. As he could not stand for any length of time he was forced to remain seated, which left him peculiarly vulnerable to getting trapped.

'What do you think of our new Festival Centre?' asked a putty-faced public servant who'd apparently had a hand in building the thing. The Adelaide Festival Centre looked like an outcrop of mushrooms designed by a minor cubist. Nestled invitingly on the banks of the Torrens, it was a smaller, cuddlier, more low-key version of the Sydney Opera House.

'It's very nice,' Teddy said politely.

'It cost about a quarter of what the Opera House cost,' the public servant said proudly. 'And it was built much more quickly. It's also far more versatile than the Opera House and the quality of the acoustics in the theatre itself are much better.'

'They must be kicking themselves in Sydney,' Teddy said mildly.

Champagne flutes and canapés circled around him. The women wore floor-length dresses which looked like spinnakers and the men wore dinner suits with elaborately frilled shirts and velvet bow ties as fat as puppy dogs. The dancers, lithe and lovely, were bright spots among the seething crowd of bores and harpies, and he found his eyes following them as they moved around the room, seeding it with their beauty, the beloved of the gods. Such delightful people they were, but so gauche and so sloppy. Soon, very soon, they would be under orders to shape up or ship out. But tonight was their night; let them enjoy themselves.

Suddenly across the hubbub he heard a voice ask with devastating clarity, 'Where is Galina tonight?'

Galina?

He turned, and discovered a sharp-edged wifey in a white Halston gown and metallic-green eye shadow talking to a crashing bore the exact size and shape of a family-sized refrigerator. Surely she couldn't mean *that* Galina?

'She couldn't come tonight, she wasn't feeling well.'

'She'll be so sorry to have missed it.'

'Ah, well. Couldn't be helped.'

And then he recognised the crashing bore. It was John Black, Mr Washing Machine, the king of locally made consumer durables.

She *did* mean that Galina.

How appalling. Although he hadn't given much thought to the matter, he had always assumed she must eventually have packed up and returned home to Europe. She had always hated Australia and she particularly hated Adelaide. It was inconceivable that after all this time she might still be here; it was like going to a desert island and stumbling upon one of those marooned Japanese soldiers who didn't know the war was over.

With Teddy the still-point at its centre, the gala crowd moved around the room with the stately precision of a Pride of Erin, and inevitably, eventually, John Black himself fetched up in front of Teddy.

'Larwood,' John drawled.

'John.'

'Long time no see.'

'Twenty-five years, in fact.'

Nine

'Has it been that long?' mused John. 'Congratulations on the appointment.'

'Thank you.' Teddy smiled acidly. 'Did you have a hand in it?'

John chortled. 'I don't have much to do with the ballet world these days.'

'What brings you here tonight then?'

'Galina and I are subscribers, of course. And I know some of the people on the board.'

'Ah.'

'Did you know Galina and I are married?'

'No, I didn't. Congratulations.'

'She couldn't come tonight. Migraine.'

'What a pity.'

'You should come and have lunch one day. I'm sure Galina would love to see you. You can talk about old times, catch up on all the gossip.'

'That would be delightful.'

John gave him a reassuring, end-of-the-conversation smile. 'It was good to see you, Larwood. Don't be a stranger now you're back.'

'Oh, I won't.'

John Black slid off into the crowd and Teddy watched him go with venomous delight. Such palpable waves of loathing and distaste! Did John Black really still hate him so much after all this time? How intriguing!

And how did Galina feel about him? He was curious to see how she had ended up after twenty-five years in purgatory. She had always been such an anomaly in this one-horse town, with her Russian cigarettes and her gravel voice, the raven-black hair pulled back off that severe and uncompromising face, her well-cut suits, her bracing no-prisoners style of criticism. She was too rigid, too controlled to be beautiful, but she was impressive, in the way a military officer is impressive. She was tough and lacquered and always so *foreign*. Had she held on to that after all this time? Or had they knocked the edges off her until she was shiny and brittle and bourgeois like all these other women, the wives?

As the official part of the evening creaked to a close, one of the dancers, Tony (blond-haired, face of an angel), came and leaned seductively over the back of his chair to murmur in his ear.

'We're all going on to another party,' he said. 'Do you want to come with us?'

Teddy looked at Tony (no, not an angel, a faun, a young Nijinsky, slanting Slavic eyes and pointed ears) and bells started to ring. For the first time that night the sap started to rise and the evening was suddenly alight with possibility.

'I'd love to,' he said.

❆ ❆ ❆

Rice-paper lightshades like harvest moons. Shaggy flokati rugs stained with wine and coffee. Home-made blinds in orange and yellow Marimekko. A record player with booming busted speakers. Winding bass lines and kicking guitars and men in platform shoes with high warbling voices. A party: no canapés, no waiters, but girls in crochet bikinis and jumpsuits, miniskirts, party dresses, boys in big flares and body shirts and jewellery, girls and boys with long hair and deep tans and healthy teeth,

Nine

dancing, smoking, drinking, flirting, stumbling about and crashing into things, laughing, passing joints. (Someone offered a joint to Teddy with a challenging air. He had a toke and passed it calmly on, rewarded with laughter.) He was the oldest person in the room by thirty or forty years but he didn't care and neither, it seemed, did they. Tony made him a throne in the lounge room — a pile of pillows from which it was almost impossible to get up — but as long as he was surrounded by a flickering, moving throng, as various and shimmering as goldfish, and someone kept filling his paper cup with nasty cheap cider, he didn't really mind. Various swan-necked girls, who he could only tell apart by the colour of their eye shadow, peppered him with questions about famous people (Did you really dance with Pavlova? — pronounced as if she were a dessert) and he unfurled all his favourite anecdotes gleefully. How charming to be among people who had never heard them before! Cee had grown sick of his stories and used to yawn obtrusively or spoil his punchlines, but now he was unstoppable — the dancers thought he was hilarious, so wild and fun and fancy-free, you'd never think he was their new boss! And always, as he rolled out tale upon tale, and the music rumped and pumped on, he kept one eye on Tony, cloven-footed Tony, as he passed back and forth, talking and smoking, changing records, passing drinks (could this be Tony's house?) and knew that Tony, too, was keeping an eye on him, pausing from time to time to laugh at one of his jokes, or just giving him a glance which said as much as a wink across the crowded room. Cee used to call him a lecherous old goat, but Cee never did understand what it was like for him: how once upon a time he had been able to make people *respond* to him, anyone, everyone, he could turn it on and off like a tap and people were helpless before *It*, whatever it was, but it gradually faded away, either with age or over-use, and as time went by he could not make people respond any more. It was like being invisible, or dead, feeling no answering *twang* from people when he smiled, and so it was not just lechery that he felt now when he saw Tony look at him from across the room, it was as if something frozen and dormant was warming and melting and coming alive, like the statue in *The Winter's Tale*, dead but now alive again, limber and quick, it was *miraculous*. And yes, it was sex, but it was not just sex, it was also something much simpler and more human than that. And the cider, which tasted like apple-flavoured paint stripper, was going to his head but the room was so warm (the kids were all dancing, shimmying and grinding) that he could not stop drinking, and even though he was beginning to loll about on the cushions like a lordly baby he was having a splendid time, and although he was shockingly drunk there wasn't much to be done about it now, was there? His stories began to get a little more risqué — the time Ninette de Valois caught him in Carabosse's chariot with a boy from the corps de ballet while a performance was going on (well, I *was* dancing the role of the Wicked Fairy. I was getting in character!) and threw him out of the company. The girls opened their jewelled eyes wide — it wasn't something that one owned up to every day — but then they laughed and so he knew it was all right, and he wondered whether to tell them about the time he met Joe Orton in the men's lavatory at the Royal Court, but his bladder was just about ready to burst, so he struggled to his feet and went

Nine

meandering off in search of the bathroom. Once he had found it, shut the door, propped himself against the wall and taken aim, he found his thoughts drifting unstoppably towards Tony. *Was* this his house? It had the look of a bachelor pad, although those cushions were cause for doubt. And there were too many different bottles lining the shower cavity for this to be a boy-only house. But perhaps there was a flatmate, one of those silken girls with the sparkling eyelids. She must be a flatmate, she couldn't be a girlfriend — he only had to look at Tony to know that. His heart fluttered madly with excitement and he decided that he must go and look for Tony *at once*. He zipped up and went out in search of him (a queue had formed for the bathroom), lobbing zig-zaggedly up the long hallway. No Tony in the kitchen. No Tony in the lounge room. No Tony in the backyard under the passionfruit vine. He turned and wobbled back, looking into the bedrooms. No Tony. No Tony. Ah!

It was a masculine room, a plain room, stripped down to the bare essentials: a bed, a wardrobe, a lamp draped with an Indian shawl that turned the light deep and red, like a bordello. Tony was there, and for some reason he had no shirt on. Teddy went in and shut the door.

'I wanted to tell you,' he said, 'how impressed I was with your dancing tonight.'

'Thanks,' said Tony, his eyes moving to the door then back to Teddy.

'You have a quality,' Teddy said, moving closer, 'that reminds me of a young Nijinsky.' (Not that he had ever seen Nijinsky dance, but never mind.)

'Didn't he go mad?' Tony asked, grinning.

'A virile quality,' Teddy said, reaching out to stroke Tony's arm, 'very powerful.'

Tony tensed, although he kept on smiling (what a trouper). Teddy wanted to reassure him that there was no need to be nervous, that everything was going to be all right, but at the same time he was suffused with such a wonderful warm sense of excitement and well-being that it did not seem necessary. Tony's slanting smile was so knowing, so wanton and so delicious, that all doubt flew away.

'I think you've got a great future ahead of you,' he said, leaned forward and kissed him full on the lips.

But as soon as he made contact he found himself in motion, a body hurtling through space, tipping and falling. Tony had dodged away from him, *had pushed him away*, throwing him off balance, and the cider and the dope and his dodgy leg sent him spiralling down, down, bouncing off the edge of the bed and onto the floor — where he was suddenly, uncontrollably and lamentably sick.

'Are you all right?' he heard someone ask, for the second time in a matter of weeks, and once again he was shamed, flattened and shamed, only this time it was so, so much worse. He felt Tony's hands under his elbows, lifting him up and plonking him onto the bed. He had tried to kiss him and been rejected. It was awful, awful. Tony flung the door open — *no more funny business* — and called, 'Could someone get me some water?' before turning back to him and saying, 'I reckon you've had too much to drink, mate.'

That blokey 'mate' made Teddy shudder. It was code — code for *hands off*.

Nine

Then the room was filled with solicitous girls, girls with glasses of water, girls offering to find him a taxi or drive him home. A smokescreen of girls, from behind which Tony made good his escape.

I am a filthy old pervert, Teddy thought to himself as clean-limbed young maidens sponged the sick from his cuffs and bathed his face.

The party was spoilt. He had made a fool of himself and it was time to go home. He allowed someone to find his walking stick, help him into a cab, convince the taxi driver that he *wouldn't* be sick again and he *did* have the fare, then close the door on him and wave him off solicitously. Tomorrow, or the next day, he would have to find Tony and apologise to him. But not now. Not now.

The last thing he glimpsed before he left the house was Tony, ardently lip-locked with a blonde little thing in a rose-coloured backless dress — just in case he hadn't got the message. He thought Tony tried to catch his eye for a split second — *sorry, grandad, but that's the way it is* — but he might have been mistaken. After all, it was late and he was very drunk.

Ten

I COME TO AUSTRALIA — MY SCHOOL IS ESTABLISHED —
I FORM A COMPANY

I come to Australia

In the summer of 1939 I was engaged for a tour by the International Russian Ballet. It was a very lengthy and arduous tour, through the Far East, New Zealand and Australia. We travelled the vast distances by steamer, and by the time we reached our destination, war had broken out. Although some of the dancers were eager to return home, our contracts were strict and could not easily be broken. We were in Melbourne when Paris fell, and we danced that night not knowing what our future held. It was our last engagement in that city and when the performance was over the company boarded a train for our next destination, Adelaide. Few of us slept that night as we rocked across the flat cold plain under a cloudless moonlit sky, and the landscape outside the window looked as bleak and featureless as the steppe. What would become of us, we wondered. Would we be recalled, would the tour be cancelled? Or would we carry on as planned, to Perth? We did not have long to wait. The notice went up that day when we reported, with red eyes and tired limbs, for company rehearsal on the stage of His Majesty's Theatre. The performance in Adelaide would be our last. Paris was in chaos and our tour was cancelled. We were stranded.

Most of the company scraped together whatever they could, sent telegrams, begged, stole and somehow got together enough money to get them home. I, too, could perhaps have done this. But what would I be returning to? I had sub-let my little apartment in Paris to another dancer before I came on the tour. What would I find when I returned? Would my things still be there, would my flat still be waiting for me? Or would the girl have fled, leaving the flat untenanted, my things lost or stolen and perhaps a stranger there in my place? Would there be work for me, a dancer getting on in years, when I went back to a Paris filled with Germans? And after all, who in their right mind wished to return to an occupied city? I remembered what Petersburg had been like after the revolution. I had fled once from starvation, from artillery, from shortages and chaos. It did not seem like a good time to return to Europe. So I stayed.

You are mad, said my friends. There is nothing for you here. Come to England, come to America, but do not stay here in this benighted place! But there was something about this country that I liked. Perhaps it was the way the air tasted. We Russians are all a little superstitious and I had a feeling that everything would be all right. I don't know what was in my mind. But the world was at war and uncertainty was everywhere and this strange and isolated country seemed as good a place as any. I am staying here, I told my friends. I will make a new life for myself. But, my friends said, you are cutting yourself off from everything you know, your culture, your home. What will you do here, how will you live? I don't know, I told them, but I will think of something.

Every so often I have been obliged to throw everything away, to leave my past behind me and start again. It is always a wrench, but good things come of it in the end. I left my childhood and my family behind when I entered the Imperial Ballet School, and I left *everything* behind when I fled my country and went to Paris. I survived those upheavals without looking back. I was sure I could do it again.

And did I regret it? Oh yes, almost daily! I had so little money, and I did not speak English. And what a place this Adelaide was for a girl from Europe! Everything here was so new, so raw, so tenuous. To me it was like a frontier town in the Wild West, cardboard façades pasted onto timber shacks so new the sap was still bubbling from the seams. And the light, the light was blinding. If you have not been to Europe you cannot understand what I am talking about. In Europe the light is gentle, it shines as if through gauze. It is diffused and golden, like the light in Baroque paintings. In these southern countries — Australia, New Zealand, Africa — it is diamond-sharp and blistering. The skies are huge and wide and very blue, and the heat in summer is unbearable. But strangest of all to me were the people, with their tall, strong, lean bodies — the men, to me, were like those of Michelangelo on the ceiling of the Sistine Chapel, massive as cart-horses — and their faces, prematurely lined and seamed by the sun, tanned like leather. The men all talked as if their jaws had been wired shut and the women sang through their noses. Compared to French women they seemed gauche and plain, and the men, even the wealthy ones, were like servants on holiday. Australia was nothing like Paris and nothing like Russia. It was not even very much like England. It was another world entirely.

But the people were not unkind. When word leaked out of our disaster, the arts lovers of Adelaide rallied around to help us. A benefit was organised to raise funds. Assistance was offered. A kind gentleman helped me to find rooms, and when I announced I was opening a dancing school of my own, the good ladies of Adelaide sent me their daughters. It was fashionable then to have your child attending Mademoiselle Koslova's Russian Dance Academy.

How strange it was for me to be a foreigner once more in an unfamiliar city, climbing the stairs to a dance studio every day. It took me back to my early days in Paris at Madame Semtsova's. I had never thought in those days that one day I too might be reduced to teaching ballet in a small room up many dusty flights of stairs. But that is how it turned out.

My girls

When I first opened my school I thought I had arrived in a ballet wasteland. There was no national school here, no professional companies. There were teachers, yes, but for the most part they were not serious. But there was at least an audience for ballet, inspired by Pavlova, who had last been in Australia in 1929, and nourished by the tours of companies such as my own International Russian Ballet. So the time was right for a serious ballet school.

I began with only a handful of girls. Some had had a little training, but it was generally of the worst sort and I had to drill them hard to remove their bad habits (derived from *musical comedy* for the most part). I knew only one way to teach: the way that I had been taught in the Imperial Ballet School, which was also the way that Madame Semtsova taught. These girls had never experienced that sort of discipline and no doubt there were some who did not care for it, but there were others who thrived on it. To my pleasure and surprise I discovered that I was a very fine teacher, something I never would have guessed while I was dancing professionally.

It was through my girls that I first began to understand the Australian character, which at first seemed so puzzling and so strange. These girls with their strong brown limbs and their good-natured approach to life were not at all Russian. There was nothing ethereal or spiritual about them. They brought with them the healthy-body healthy-mind attitude of the physical culture academy. The people in the office below my studio never ceased complaining about the thump-thump-thump through the floor. Are you training a herd of young elephants up there? they would say, exasperated. Tread lightly, girls, tread lightly, I would say. Try and imagine you are a sylph. There was nothing sylph-like about my girls in those early days.

On showing off

One of the things I did not understand, and have never understood, is the Australian distaste for *putting yourself forward,* or *showing off.* I did not understand how you could consider a career as a performer when you found it repugnant to step forward and say: *Here I am. Look at me. I am the best.*

Australians have a weird obsession with modesty, with *not rising above the pack.* It is a terrible insult to say that a person *has tickets on himself* — that is to say, has too high an opinion of themselves. This national habit of self-deprecation ruined many of my girls, who had everything going for them except confidence. I remember one girl, whose name was Betty — a lovely expressive little dancer. She always put her heart and soul into everything she did. I thought she was very promising (although admittedly she was a little on the short side) but there was something about her that the other girls could not stand. They started mimicking her behind her back, exaggerating her expressive ways. Her classmates disliked her because they thought she was *showing off.* Betty cared more about being liked by the other girls than she did about her dancing, and over time the quality of her work diminished, becoming cramped and joyless. Eventually she left ballet, all her early promise squandered. She was not the only one I lost this way. I found this very sad, and puzzling too.

The senior class

I came up with a solution to this problem when I was in my second year of teaching. I decided I would start a special class, to be called the senior class, for those girls who were serious about dancing and who were talented enough to contemplate a career as a professional dancer. This class could be joined by invitation only, and it allowed me to separate the real dancers from the amateurs. In this class, there were no problems such as Betty had experienced. These girls were all show-offs and didn't think there was anything wrong with it. As word got out, my other students began begging me to let them join the senior class. This was very pleasing, for it had the unexpected side effect of making them work harder. But I was determined to keep numbers small so that I could work intensively with the girls I had chosen. Twelve is a good number for a class. Any more than that becomes too difficult to manage. And my studio at that time was not large.

One of the mothers once accused me of being unfair and elitist (I had not let her little darling join the senior class). She told me it was very wrong of me to choose some girls and not others. She thought all of them deserved a fair go and that it was wrong to have two classes. Of course it is unfair and elitist, I said. In ballet, only the best succeed. Surely that should be obvious.

On concerts

At the Imperial Ballet School we did not give concerts. From an early age we appeared on the stage of the Maryinsky, so it was not considered necessary. I soon learned, however, that in Australia ballet concerts are essential, not just for the little darlings, but also for the loving parents who want to see what their hard-earned pennies have bought.

the Snow Queen

Some dancing schools put on a performance at the drop of a hat: not just at the end of every term, but also at every conceivable public event, from the church fête to the local Christmas pageant. When first I saw one of these displays I was *flabbergasted*. If that is all that is required, I told myself, I will have no difficulty putting on a show.

I return to the stage

After much hesitation and doubt, I decided that I would appear upon the stage with my pupils. I performed the *grand pas de deux* from The Nutcracker with my dear friend Andrei Pavlovich Volkonsky as my partner. (Like me, Andrei had arrived in Australia with the International Russian Ballet and had decided to remain here after he met an Australian girl.) I think it is only fair to say that our performance was the great success of the night. Andrei and I were loudly applauded, and could perhaps have come back for an encore had we prepared one. But it had been a long night for the little ones and so we took our bows and allowed everyone to go home.

My first concert was a great success and the following day a very complimentary notice appeared in the newspaper. Over the next week a number of the parents came to me and suggested that I should consider a return to the stage. The consensus seemed to be that my senior girls — although they were young — could form the *corps* of a ballet company, with myself as ballerina and Andrei as *premier danseur*. At first I dismissed the idea as absurd, but the more I thought about it, the more it began to appeal. Although I knew little about producing, it did seem possible that a small classical ballet company could make a living from touring. The school would provide me with properly trained dancers, and if the company was a failure I could always return to teaching. What did I have to lose?

The Koslova Ballet

I decided my company would be a classical company in the old style. Lacking as I did the support of the Tsar and all his wealth, there could be no question of lavish costumes and casts of two hundred dancers! But the heart of the ballet does not lie in spectacle — this much I had learned from Diaghilev. Spectacle must always be secondary to the purity of the dancing. I could not mount the great story ballets as I had known them, but I could present excerpts and highlights, the kind of dancing which had been a staple of Pavlova's tours. Act Two of *Swan Lake* was not beyond my grasp. There was an audience for such things if they were beautifully performed, and I would see to it that they were. And I hoped that in time I would be able to present the glories of the international repertoire as they should be seen, in full.

My little family

I cannot tell you how delightful it was to be part of a permanent company again (well, I say permanent — in fact it was not, because I could not afford to pay my dancers full time). I had lived alone for many years, taking one touring job after another, living out of a suitcase, never in one place for very long, joining this company and that company. It was an itinerant existence, and it was not easy to make friends, or to keep them. The atmosphere of a tour, when you are constantly on the move and constantly living at close quarters with others, creates a certain false intimacy. But it ends as soon as the tour ends, and frequently I was glad of it. With my own company, however, things were very different.

How well I remember our first tour! Many of my girls had never left South Australia before and were half-convinced that they would be captured by white slavers as soon as they arrived in sinful Sydney. Everything was new to them: new streets, new theatres, new lodgings. Although I was scarcely less ignorant than they, I had to pretend that I knew what I was doing and knew exactly where I was going. I often felt like a mother hen, herding my twittering charges on and off trains, trams and buses, in and out of dressing rooms, hotels and boarding houses. It had never occurred to me that the greatest part of my task in running a ballet company would lie in soothing and placating and managing and controlling a gaggle of over-excited young women. (I should point out that on our first tour there was precisely one male in the company, Andrei.) This was more difficult than I had expected and I found I had to draw on previously untapped resources of patience and calm.

There are a hundred tales I could tell about that tour, and the many that followed, but I will allow a small taste to suffice.

Although I had given my girls strict instructions that they were to bring only one suitcase and one overnight bag — only as much as they could carry, in other words — Laura turned up on the platform of the railway station with a suitcase, three hatboxes and a steamer trunk. I couldn't *possibly* travel with anything less, she insisted. Her father was with her and offered

Ten

to write me a cheque to pay for porters to carry all of Laura's luggage. I made her repack her bag right there on the platform.

Sylvia had brought with her only two dresses — one of which she was wearing — and had filled the rest of her suitcase with books. The other girls laughed at her but when those long train journeys from city to city began she soon found herself extremely popular.

Posy was a cardsharp. She taught all the girls to play poker and then proceeded to win from them money, silk stockings, nylons and anything else her unfortunate companions were willing to risk. Eventually the girls got wise to her and would only play for matches, although she once won fifty pounds from an unwary GI from Kentucky, who couldn't believe that Posy's guileless face might conceal a mind like a steel trap.

Amy gave me the most trouble. She had had a very careful upbringing and, as a consequence, she was perfectly wild. Her mother and father had delivered her into my hands with many tears, demanding endless reassurances that I would take care of her moral welfare, keep her away from bad influences and see to it that she went to church every Sunday. Naturally enough, Amy had other ideas. No sooner had the train pulled away from the platform than she was off down the train, flirting with a carriage full of soldiers. Wherever we went, if there were men and dancing and men and drink and men and cigarettes and men and trouble and men to be found, she would be there, raring to go. Amy was always out on the town after a performance, always surrounded by a gaggle of admirers, and always came home staggering under the weight of the chocolates and stockings and cigarettes and jewellery and dolls and stuffed toys her admirers gave her. She smoked the cigarettes, shared the chocs and the stockings, and gave the dolls and toys away to orphanages. The jewellery she kept. She was wild, Amy, but she was good-hearted. She reminded me a little of my old friend Natasha, but Amy was not interested in finding a husband. She was having too much fun as a single girl.

The girls were divided loosely into two types: the wild ones (Amy was their ringleader) and the quiet ones. The quiet ones, like studious Sylvia, read books, went to the pictures and knitted things for our boys overseas. They were never any trouble, always came to class on time and were never too ill to perform and, fortunately for me, they were in the majority. The wild ones soon learned that what they did in their own time was their own business, but if they missed a class, or worse still, a performance, there would be serious consequences. Amy once spent an entire evening vomiting in the lavatory when she should have been onstage. When I tackled her about it afterwards, she insisted she'd had a bad chop for tea, even though I knew she'd been out until dawn the night before. (The landlady had explained to me indignantly that she'd come stumbling in drunk at breakfast time in front of other paying customers — *I run a respectable establishment, no room for sluts and harlots*, etc etc.) I docked Amy's pay and told her in front of the whole company that if anything like that were to happen again she'd be put on the first train home. This did not mean the girls stopped having fun, of course, but they took care not to get caught. And they were always ready to perform.

We had endless trouble with lodgings. Landladies were always extremely strict about meal times and would not, under any circumstances, permit any changes to their schedule. Breakfast was served between seven and eight, dinner between twelve and one, and tea between six and seven. Time and again I explained that the girls had to be at the theatre at seven in the evening and did not come home until well after midnight, which meant that they could not be there for breakfast or tea (and on matinee days they often missed dinner too). The landladies were usually immovable on this subject, so I was forced to make a practice of going out and buying large quantities of bread, ham, cheese and apples, so that the girls might not starve to death.

On one memorable occasion we took lodgings in a place in Brisbane that turned out to be a brothel. (I had wondered why the rooms were so cheap.) Men were knocking on our doors at all hours of the night, and little Lucinda got a terrible fright when she let one of them in. The screams were audible from one end of the establishment to the other. When I arrived to see what the trouble was I found her holding a startled gentleman at bay with a Mason and Pearson hairbrush. I sent him on his way with a flea in his ear and then instructed all my girls to lock their doors. We left the following morning, very short of sleep.

It was not all fun and games, however. The younger girls were often homesick and frightened, and they looked to me for reassurance, especially when things went wrong. Girls like Amy could look after themselves, but there were others who were less confident and less experienced, and these girls got themselves into difficulties with men. Catherine, normally a very quiet girl, was coaxed out on the town by some of the others and acquired a very strange and persistent admirer. Anyone else would have told him to clear off but Catherine was much too polite, and as a consequence he started hanging around the theatre and then at our lodgings. When he tried one night to break into her room, Catherine at last came to me and told me the whole story. I was outraged and went storming outside, where I found him hovering in the backyard, fingering someone's underthings on the washing line (not ours, as chance would have it). I screamed at him in Russian, French and English and made it quite clear that his intentions were unwanted and that if he came back again I would shoot him. There are advantages in sounding like a temperamental foreigner. People will believe you are capable of just about anything.

One of my girls got herself into another sort of trouble — the oldest sort. She was at her wits' end when she came to me: she didn't want the child, she didn't want to marry the father (who, in turn, didn't want to marry her) and most of all she didn't want her family to know. After twenty years in the theatre, this situation was not unknown to me (although fortunately I had not been in it myself) and I knew what had to be done. I had a chat with the unwilling father and managed to make him see sense, of a kind — that is, I extracted some money from him — and then I found a doctor. We were lucky — the doctor was a good man, no backyard butcher, and the girl was fine.

I know there are some people who would consider this shocking, but at the time it seemed like the only thing to be done. It has never seemed fair to me that a man may take his pleasure where he will and walk away, but a girl, who may be just as ambitious as he is, with all her life ahead of her, is expected to bear the burden of shame if she has the child, or guilt if she gets rid of it. When my girl came to me, tearful and desperate, and begged me to get her out of this mess, I truly felt that the only thing I could do was to help her, as I would have wanted someone to help me if I was in her situation. Perhaps I should have encouraged her to keep the child and live with the consequences. But I did not have the heart to do it.

Kschessinska's child

In 1902 Mathilde Kschessinska gave birth to her only child. She was two months short of her thirtieth birthday, she was unmarried, and she was one of the most beloved ballerinas in the Imperial Ballet. Fortunately for Kschessinska, the father of her child was a grand duke and he gave her the kind of protection which only money and position can buy. She danced right through the fifth month of pregnancy, only retiring from the stage when she could no longer turn sideways for fear of displaying her conspicuous bump. She returned to the stage exactly two months after the birth, and continued to dance for another fifteen years.

Wartime

The war made many things difficult — there were shortages and scares, mini-submarines in Sydney Harbour and air raids over Darwin — but in many ways, the war years were good to a young ballet company. Before the war, Australia had been part of a well-established touring circuit which brought all the great stars from Europe and America to audiences in this country. But once the war began, the tours stopped. There were no more ships and the stars could not come here. This was a great boon for local performers — we did not have to compete with imported stars for the attention and the hard-earned cash of our audiences. The pressures of wartime meant that people were hungry for entertainment — boys on R&R, girls doing war work, all of them with money in their pockets and more freedom than they'd ever had before, spending every day as if it were their last. Audiences flocked to us, as they flocked to anything and everything else. We toured twice a year during the war, always with a different program, and each tour was more successful than the one before.

This is not to say it was easy, however. My struggles with English, my nationality and my sex all caused many difficulties. Because of my accent I was often accused of being a spy (even after Russia entered the war) and on several occasions I had to explain myself to the police. They always let me go once they understood who I was, but it was very frightening nonetheless.

It was also difficult to find male dancers for the company. Australia simply did not have trained men, and whenever I found a young fellow with an inclination in that direction, which was not often, he was usually snapped up by the war effort. I was fortunate that I had my dear old partner Andrei to rely upon, for otherwise it would have been completely impossible, but he was already some years older than myself and I worried about what I would do when he decided to retire.

I thought I had found a solution to this problem when I discovered a young man called Archie. He was the brother of one of my students and would often accompany her to lessons. At first he merely sat in a corner and watched, but I noticed that his feet would bump and his hands would twitch in time with the music, and he always followed the action very keenly, and so at last I invited him to join in. He was only sixteen at the time, and rather afraid of what *the fellas* might say, but he had a knack for it, and once he began he came on in leaps and bounds. He was strong and enthusiastic and could jump like a steeplechaser, and I was filled with excitement. I dreamed of turning him into a star and began to plan my season around him, but the very moment he turned eighteen he joined up and I lost him. (Fortunately for both of us, he survived the war unscathed and rejoined the company once he was demobbed.)

My single greatest difficulty, however, was my sex. In wartime there were many women who had to fend for themselves, taking the jobs of the men who had gone overseas. But after the war, when the men came back, all those women were supposed to put their jobs aside and go quietly home again. No one could understand why I was still running the company. They would not believe I was the person in charge, they always asked to speak to the manager. I was ripped off many times, because they thought a stupid foreigner, a stupid woman, would not notice. The battles I fought when they cheated me! But nowhere did I get any sympathy. Everyone told me I should just get a manager and save myself all the bother.

But I knew I could run the company perfectly well on my own, and I refused to put my affairs into the hands of some man, as if I was incapable, when I knew perfectly well I was not incapable. I decided I would find someone to stand in for me, a figurehead, a man who would come along to meetings and sign his name to letters and so forth, and leave me alone to run my company as I saw fit. The person I chose was Teddy.

Eleven

Once he had been demobbed, Teddy found himself looking about once again for something to do. Opportunities were few for a young male dancer, and even though the war was over, there were still none of the luxuries of life to be had, which Teddy considered the only necessities! So he decided to go home and visit his family for the first time in many years.

The family were delighted to see him and were amazed at how well he'd done for himself in London. Teddy met all the nephews and nieces he'd heard so much about but never seen and quickly made himself a favourite with all the small fry!

While he was in Adelaide he was introduced to a woman who was to play a big part in the next phase of his career: Miss Galina Koslava. Miss Koslava had danced with the Ballets Russes and had set up her own ballet company in Australia. She couldn't believe her luck when she laid eyes on Teddy: she had had great difficulty finding male dancers since her former partner had retired, and here all of a sudden was a genuine ballet star! She immediately invited Teddy to join her company and would not take no for an answer, no matter how many times Teddy tried to explain he was only there on holiday. Eventually her begging and pleading got the better of him and he gave in. Soon enough, Teddy was touring the country as a guest artist, performing all the lead roles he had made his own in London before the war. It was all the more satisfying for him because he was at last showing his countrymen what he could do!

But Miss Koslava's company did not just perform classical ballets, they also did new works. Until Teddy came along, these were mostly dances put together by the ladies of the company. Teddy had never thought of turning his hand to choreography before, but when Miss Koslava suggested he should try it, he threw himself into the task with gusto! His first piece was a classical solo which he created for himself. The first time he performed it onstage, he received a standing ovation. He was a natural!

Miss Koslava begged him to create more ballets for the company, and he gladly complied. It was at this time that he began to feel it was important to create dance works which were relevant to Australian audiences. His second ballet was a powerful symbolic work called 'Terra Australis', in which the spirit of Australia, danced by a young ballerina, is torn between her first love, the Aboriginal, and a new suitor, the Explorer. After a tender duet between Australia and the Aboriginal, the curious young girl is tempted by the Explorer, who gradually wins her love. When the Aboriginal sees them together he goes

Eleven

into a jealous rage and attacks the Explorer. The Explorer fights back and in the struggle the Aboriginal is killed. Australia and the Explorer mourn his passing, before dancing a final duet of joy in their newfound love. 'Terra Australis' caused a sensation when it premiered, attracting widespread praise for its daring use of Australian themes and motifs. It was the first of many triumphs for Teddy.

But the bright lights of London beckoned, and so, after two years with the company, Teddy bid a fond farewell to Miss Koslava and returned to London.

Sylvia Sampson-Harris, ***Dancing Feet: The Life of Edward Larwood,*** **Angus & Robertson, 1974**

Twelve

TEDDY JOINS THE COMPANY — ON CHOREOGRAPHY

I meet Teddy

It seems hard to believe now, but I chose Teddy because I thought he was malleable.

He came to see me at my studio, where I had been taking company class. He mooched in, so nonchalant, so beautiful in his camel overcoat and his London tailoring. He was an exotic flower in this town, in those times. He had danced with Sadler's Wells, and his name and face were known to me for he had been much talked about before the war, although I had not met him.

'Mademoiselle Koslova,' he said, in his very cultivated, very English drawl, 'Edward Larwood, at your service.' He kissed my hand. There was not much hand-kissing to be had in Australia in 1946 and I was charmed.

'I am pleased to make your acquaintance, Mr Larwood,' I replied. 'But I am surprised to find you in this corner of the world. What brings you here?'

'I've come home to visit Mother,' he said, in his humorous way.

'You, Mr Larwood? An Australian boy?'

'I'm afraid so. And please call me Teddy.'

He was by then past thirty but he seemed younger. Teddy was always precious about his youth and desperate to hold on to it. The name was part of it, and he always cultivated a boyish manner. He had face-lifts later on.

'What can I do for you, Teddy?' I asked, thinking perhaps he wanted to join my class.

'I was rather hoping you could give me a job.'

'What sort of job?'

'A dancing job, obviously.'

Well, my heart jumped for joy when he said this.

'I thought you had a job,' I said. 'With Sadler's Wells.'

'Miss de Valois hasn't asked me back.'

'Why not?'

'I got into rather a sticky situation with one of the dancers. We'd been getting along famously and I thought we had an understanding, but it turned out I thought it was one thing and she thought it was another and ... well, there was a dreadful misunderstanding and she complained to Miss de Valois and that was the end of that.'

I remember the look on his face as he waited to see how I

would react — like a naughty schoolboy caught with his fingers in the jam.

'I trust there would be no repeat performance if I were to give you a job,' I said.

His smile came out, bright and caressing all at once, a heartbreaking smile, and I think it was the smile, more than anything, that convinced me.

'Believe me, *Mademoiselle*, I would comport myself with the utmost discretion if you gave me a job. In fact you've got nothing to worry about on that score. I'm through with love. From now on I'm going to live for my art.'

I did not believe it for a moment. But I gave him the job.

Now, I wonder what on earth I was doing taking on someone like Teddy, but at the time I had several good reasons. First, Teddy was a beautiful dancer. No male dancer in the country could match him. In fact he was one of the finest dancers of his generation, in this country or any other. His technique was never strong, but he made up for it with his dramatic qualities and the beauty of his expression. Secondly, I was in desperate need of a partner. Of course I still had Andrei, but he was five years older than I and getting fat, and although his artistry was undeniable, audiences had started to snigger when he walked on in his tights, and he was getting tired of it all. For my sake he kept going, but he could not have gone on for much longer. So Teddy's arrival came at exactly the right time. And thirdly, then as now, Australia and its audiences were very nationalistic and they wanted to see home-grown talent. I knew it would make good publicity if I hired their 'local boy made good'. So Teddy was like a gift from God.

And as for his private life, when I met him he seemed transparent and open and honest. He had confessed his disgrace to me and laid himself bare. Ballet training teaches obedience and I thought I could guide him. How could I know then that Teddy was not the kind of dancer I was used to, but the other kind, the mad and bad kind, the maniac, the genius? (I am not sure that Teddy was ever a genius. But I think he wanted to be, and that is troublesome enough.) And although for the sake of publicity we would advertise him as a local boy, Teddy was not local. He had gone away many years earlier because this country could not hold him, it could not sustain or understand him. If he had not leapt out of the nest he would have been thrown out. He aspired to a wider world of art and civilisation, the world that I knew, the world of European culture. He had been a part of the London ballet scene for ten years, he knew painters and composers, he understood what words like 'modernism' meant. I cannot describe what a *wasteland* this distant country was then, how unfamiliar, and how lonely I had been, cut off from all the things that mattered to me. When Teddy walked into my classroom, he brought with him the savour of all the old familiar things I had lost. He was a zephyr from the old world, and I could breathe again.

But all those reasons, although they were good ones, were not the real reason I hired Teddy. His smile was the reason. It's not that I had romantic ideas about him. But there are some people who are incandescent, who make you feel better when they are near you. He was one of those people. He was like a slap in the face, a jolt of electricity. He made me feel alive in a way that I had not felt for many years. So of course I seized him at once.

Twelve

Teddy joins the company

It is difficult to describe what a galvanising effect Teddy had, not just upon me but on all of the company. He had a charisma which was undeniable, but which is quite impossible to describe. It was in his looks, his voice, the way he held himself; it was in the quality of his attention. He had a way of listening that made you seem more interesting to yourself. He was a born flirt, a born flatterer — he could not help himself. But the truth was, he was very good at it. He was, in fact, almost irresistible.

Some dancers are interested only in ballet, but that was never Teddy's way. He loved to keep abreast of all the newest trends in art and music and literature. He received all sorts of magazines from overseas and ordered in crate-loads of books (I don't think he ever finished them, but he started them). There had been, I think, an older and more cultured lover in Teddy's past, who had taken him in hand and given him a cultural education. Teddy now began to do the same thing with me.

'You should be ashamed of how little you know!' he would cry. 'You, a serious artist! Do you know anything about anything outside of ballet?'

'Of course I do,' I said, although I didn't.

'You probably think Picasso is a man who once did some décor for Diaghilev,' Teddy said.

'Isn't he?' I replied. My ignorance was a great joke between us.

It was Teddy who encouraged me to read. He played me classical music too, and took me to art exhibitions. I never cared for modern art, but Teddy loved it all, as long as it was new and it annoyed people. (I have often thought that if I was born too late, Teddy was born too early.)

Almost from the beginning, Teddy had big plans for the company. He was never content to be the hired help, turning up for rehearsals and dancing on cue. He didn't just work for the company, he adored the whole idea of it. Although it was always my company and he respected my decisions (until the end, that is, when it all started to go wrong), he was always tackling me, arguing, enthusing, rehearsing his ideas for what an Australian company could be.

'We are the first professional ballet company in Australia,' he would say to me. 'We have a chance to do something really innovative.'

'I have no interest in innovation,' I said, 'this country does not need innovation, what it needs is *standards*.'

'But if we set out to be a true classical company, we can never be anything but a second-rate copy,' Teddy said. 'We can never compete with the Russian Ballet or the Danish Royal Ballet or any of those other companies. They have centuries of tradition that define who and what they are. We have no traditions at all, we're building on sand.'

'That is why we must give them a tradition. The best tradition. The Russian tradition.'

'But we're not Russian. We're Australian.'

'In the Ballets Russes there were many dancers who were not Russian, it did not matter, they danced in the Russian style.'

'The Ballets Russes was a Russian company with a Modernist sensibility and a French name,' Teddy said. 'It was a company with an identity and a vision and a strong guiding hand.'

'Are you saying I do not have a strong guiding hand?'

'No, of course not, that's not what I mean. The Ballets Russes was an amazing company because it took the best elements of a great tradition and married it with something entirely unprecedented, modern and new. This country is so young it seems to me we've got no choice but to try and do something similar.'

'I loathe experimentation for experimentation's sake.'

'I'm not talking about experimentation, I'm talking about building our own tradition. One that takes the best elements from the past and adapts it to our circumstances, our situation. Look out the window,' Teddy would say, 'can you imagine any Wilis out there? Any Sylphs?'

'If you mention black swans to me one more time —'

'This is a new country, a young country. We don't want to be mired in the past. We should be looking to the future.'

'Without its traditions ballet has no future,' I replied.

'For a minute or two,' he argued, 'back in the twenties, ballet looked like it might have come back from the dead. For once it was actually in the vanguard, it was new, it was radical, it was exciting. I don't want to see it turning back into a dreary museum piece.'

'Ballet is about the perfection of technique and beautiful interpretations of the classics,' I said.

'What is art?' Teddy would ask. 'Tell me. What do you think art is for?'

'Art exists to create beautiful and uplifting things. It is there to elevate the spirit and to make life more attractive.'

'That's not art, that's wallpaper.'

'Then what do you think art is for?'

'Art,' he said, 'shows us the world in new ways. It lets us look at things on an angle, so that we see things as we have never seen them before. It shows us the things that have been right under our noses, so close we can't see them, even though they're in plain view. Art allows you to ask the question: who am I? What can I make of myself, what can I become?'

'If you can put all that in a ballet,' I said, 'you're a better mime than I am.'

'It's the task of artists,' Teddy said, 'to pose questions and to imagine possibilities. Artists dream a country into being, and in a new country like this one, those questions are even more urgent. It's our job to explore, to uncover the real Australia, to tell the truth and to show the world who we really are.'

'You're an expat and I'm a Russian. What do we know about the real Australia?'

'You see things more clearly when you're on the outside,' Teddy said.

With such arguments as these he gradually wore down my resistance, until I agreed to focus more of the company's activity on the development and presentation of new modern ballets. But Teddy was not the first choreographer to work for my company. Nor was he the best. That honour belongs to Posy Foster.

Posy

Posy Foster was sixteen when she first came to me, and a most talented dancer (and poker player). She was an original member of my senior class and one of the first to join the company. She

Twelve

had dark eyes and red hair, and a most regrettable habit of sun-baking. I have never seen a dancer with so many freckles. (When she joined the company I had to be very strict with her. In the world of the romantic ballet, I told her, there is only moonlight. A sunburnt sylph will never be seen on *my* stage.) She came to see me one day after class, very shy and apprehensive.

'Miss Koslova, can I talk to you about something?' she asked.

'Of course,' I replied.

'It's about the concert,' she said. (This was in 1941.) 'I was wondering ... you see the thing is ...'

I was growing impatient. 'Please to spit it out, young lady, whatever it is.'

Posy took a deep breath. 'I've made up a dance,' she said, 'and I was wondering if I might perform it at the concert.'

I was not filled with confidence. She was only a slip of a girl and I had no reason to expect she had any talent in the choreographic line. But I thought I should at least see what she could do.

'You will show me this dance,' I said.

With great eagerness she ran to the changing room and came back with a gramophone record. So I put it on and watched as she took up her first position.

What a surprise I had that day!

The dance Posy performed for me was strictly academic in style, without any of the regrettable lapses into the contemporary idioms (whether jazz, tap, modern, musical comedy, etc) that are so common today, particularly in the young. It was virtuosic without being acrobatic. It was a perfectly balanced dialogue between the music and the movement. It can be too easy in choreography either to follow every beat and movement within the music, resulting in something which feels hackneyed or mechanical, or to resist the music, ignoring its natural highs and lows, and thus producing something odd and disjointed. Posy's piece was only three or four minutes long, but it avoided these pitfalls. She had choreographed something which fitted neatly within her abilities, and she performed it beautifully. I was captivated.

'You have a talent for choreography,' I said when she had finished. 'I would be very pleased if you would perform this dance at the concert.'

'Thank you, Miss Koslova,' she cried, her eyes shining.

And that was how I found my first choreographer.

Bronislava Nijinska

Serge Diaghilev worked with five major choreographers during his lifetime. Some had never choreographed before and only began the work through his encouragement. Those five choreographers were Michel Fokine (who had formerly made ballets for the Imperial Theatres), Vaslav Nijinsky, Bronislava Nijinska, Leonide Massine and George Balanchine. Of these five, Bronislava Nijinska was the only woman. (It has always been surprising to me that in a field where women are so prominent, there are so few female choreographers.) Nijinska was the sister of the great Vaslav and a dancer with the Diaghilev company. Nijinska was a pioneer of Modernism, with her own ideas about the future of ballet. She clashed frequently with Diaghilev over issues of artistic control. On Diaghilev's stage, the look of a ballet was often determined by the designer, not the choreographer. Nijinska did not accept this and insisted that the vision of the designer must be secondary to the needs of the dancer and the demands of the choreography. There would be no heavy sackcloth costumes or pieces of ambulant sculpture on her stage, no indeed! Nijinska worked for a short time with Diaghilev, creating for him only a few ballets, but it is now acknowledged that two of those works — *Les Noces* and *Les Biches* — were among the most important of the ballets created for the Diaghilev company.

Repertoire

Naturally, with my tiny group of dancers and threadbare resources, I could not consider mounting full-length story ballets. (I did manage a *Swan Lake* once, with chamber orchestra, in 1944, but the cost almost bankrupted me and I could not afford to reassemble the company again until after VJ Day.) Like Diaghilev before me, I was obliged to mount triple bills of one-act ballets instead, filled out with *divertissements*. I was very fortunate in having an excellent memory and could reproduce the choreography of many of the ballets I had danced during my long career. These ballets formed the backbone of our repertoire. Posy also created a number of ballets which were deservedly popular with audiences. But it could not be said that new choreography was a real feature in the life of the company until Teddy came along.

the Snow Queen

On becoming a choreographer

Teddy and Posy followed very different paths towards becoming a choreographer. They were like the hare and the tortoise (although this comparison is a little unfair to Posy, who did in fact work quite quickly) but it gives a clear picture of their approach, which was all about haste versus patience.

Teddy always lacked discipline (you could see it in his technique). He resented authority and loathed being told what to do. He became bored easily. Many times during his career he gave up dancing to do something else — here acting, there directing. He made films. He appeared on television. Always, eventually, he would come back to dance, but I do not believe he ever really had the right temperament for ballet. He could not submerge himself into a larger whole — the seamless unity of the *corps de ballet* was not for him. Of course, he was fortunate: he had talent, and he was a man. It is always easier for a man to rise in the ballet world, there is so little competition. Teddy was never forced to learn patience.

But apart from this, there was another, much greater difference between Teddy and Posy, and that was Teddy's faith in his own talent. Whereas Posy was always modest, cautious and reluctant to blow her own trumpet, Teddy believed his talent (his genius?) was so enormous that he could do most things better than most people. He was not content to stick with dancing, because he knew he could become a great choreographer (or painter, or poet, or composer, or architect, or *anything*) if he could only find the time to try his hand at it. He longed to produce a ballet with music by Larwood,

Twelve

choreography by Larwood, scenario by Larwood, design by Larwood, conducted by Larwood through a skilful use of his left toe while he danced the leading role. In fact he never brought any such thing to fruition, for he lacked the necessary ability to see something through to the bitter end. They say that creativity is ten per cent inspiration and ninety per cent perspiration. Inspiration was Teddy's speciality, but perspiration did not suit him at all.

So what were Teddy's abilities as a choreographer? Did he have some talent? Or did his ambition surpass his ability? At a distance of some years, I must admit that he was, at best, erratic. Every month he would appear at the choreographic workshop (one of his many innovations) with some new piece or other, and since Teddy was very popular among the company, and quite an effective performer of his own work, his pieces were usually well received. I'll say this for him, he was never short of ideas, but he was always so slapdash in his execution that he rarely managed to carry anything through to a satisfying conclusion. He also lacked a sense of compositional propriety, so that his ballets would leap stylistically from the ultra-modern to the dreamily neo-romantic, often to jarring effect. For example, one of his early ballets was based on the affection Australians have for their football teams — a bizarre subject for a ballet in my view, and even more bizarre in the treatment. The first scene showed a brutish husband abusing his shrewish wife before going off with the boys to a game. The second scene represented the football match, danced in stylised fashion by the men of the company. The third, climactic scene featured a love duet between the football fan and a ballerina representing The Spirit of the Club in a tutu, *pointe* shoes and the colours of the Norwood football club (navy and red, complete with striped socks). The dancers thought this was *très amusant* but I was certainly not going to let it appear on any program of mine.

Eventually his works reached a sufficient standard that I began to include them in our programs. Critical opinion was mixed: Teddy's dancing was always praised, but it was observed by more than one critic that the stylishness of his performance was masking the thinness of his material. Nonetheless, I stood by him and supported him. Teddy had managed to convince me that the long-term health of the company depended on us having a pool of experienced and talented people to draw upon. How ironic it seems to me now that I should have been so concerned about planning for the future! Although I did not know it then, Teddy's choreographic ambitions would mark the beginning of the end for my company.

Thirteen

The changing room was filled to overflowing with girls, girls, girls, classical girls in plain black leotards and buns, jazzy girls all tits'n'teeth, rows of anxious mothers and anxious teachers, and a smattering, just a smattering, of thin weedy boys. They must have done the numbers and realised they had an even chance of getting in. No wonder they looked so smug. Every girl in South Australia who'd ever gone to ballet school seemed to have turned up, and at least half of them stood absolutely no chance — he could have told them not to even bother changing their shoes — but an open audition was an open audition and they all had to be given their little moment. He knew just how the Prince in *Cinderella* must have felt.

Smothering a yawn, he scanned the room, and out of the sea of lightly tanned limbs and kohl-rimmed eyes, a familiar face jumped out at him. Two cheeks as round as apples sat in the middle of a face which was otherwise clean-boned, straight-lined. The eyes, sharp and penetrating, were dark brown, and the hair, once red, was turning a sandy pepper and salt, cropped in a gamine cut. Posy.

She must be nearing fifty, and her figure was starting to thicken, but she looked smart and independent in flat shoes and a tailored suit. She had a gaggle of girls with her — presumably her pupils — and Teddy found himself assailed once again by the strangeness of it all. After so many years, that Posy should still be here, teaching. It was incredible. She saw him then and waved, and he waved back. He watched as she spoke briefly to her girls and then crossed the room to greet him. Her step was still light and vibrant.

'Hello, Teddy.'

'I can't believe you're still here.'

'Neither can I sometimes.'

'Are you a parent or a teacher?' he asked, although he was fairly certain she was not a parent.

'Teacher. Those are my girls over there.'

She pointed, smiling, and Teddy glanced at the clutch of nervous faces turned in their direction.

'Do you have many places in the company?' Posy asked.

'I'll take all the boys you've got,' Teddy said.

She laughed. 'Some things never change.'

They were silent for a moment.

'You look well, Teddy.'

'So do you.'

'I look mature,' she said, and laughed again.

Thirteen

'You're not the only one.'

'You look just the same. Apart from the snow on the roof.'

'Oh, that. I dye it, you know.'

They smiled at each other. He was remembering how much he used to like Posy in the old days. She was always so calm in the face of hysterics, so relaxed and self-contained, so quick to laugh. It was a rare quality in a dancer.

'What happened to you?' he asked. 'How did you end up here?'

'I joined the Borovansky Ballet and danced with them for a few years. I did quite well for myself and went overseas, but then I had knee problems and couldn't dance for a long time. When I came back the work had dried up, so I followed Miss Koslova's lead and opened a ballet school.'

'You didn't think about moving to a bigger city?'

'My family are here.'

'And are you still making ballets?'

'Who would I make them for?' Posy asked wryly. 'I'm a lady teacher from Adelaide. Who'd give me a chance?'

❈ ❈ ❈

The first time he really took notice of Posy was when he saw her name on one of the company's posters: '*La Mer*, a ballet in one act by Posy Foster'. He had been with the company for nearly six months, but until that moment she had been nothing more than a part of the moving throng. Now, suddenly, he was intrigued.

'Is she any good?' he asked.

'Miss Koslova seems to think so.'

It had not occurred to him until that moment that one could be a dancer and a choreographer at the same time. But once the idea had been presented to him, he could not leave it alone. Choreography seemed like the answer to a question he hadn't quite been able to formulate — it was a solution to his restlessness, his boredom with ballet, the frustration of being told what to do. He had uncovered a desire which he hadn't even known was in him, the desire to create, and once discovered it was all-consuming. He felt like the boy who had everything, discovering something new to want. It was exhilarating; it was bliss.

He sought Posy out.

'How did you start?' he asked.

'I went to Miss Koslova and showed her a dance I'd made up and it went on from there.'

She was so artless, Posy. She did not choreograph, she 'made up a dance'.

'Do you think she'd be interested if I showed her something?'

'I'm sure she would.'

Suddenly his days had structure. He was filled with eager purpose. He pored through art books, listened endlessly to music. He read reviews of new dance from London and Paris and tried to imagine what the ballets had looked like. Everything became grist to his mill. A ballet could lie anywhere: in a look, a thought, a story, a poem. It could lie inside a flute concerto, a chorale, a collection of Baroque variations, a jazz record. He thought about every ballet he had ever been in. He thought about the way that the most interesting ballets invented

Thirteen

for themselves a new language, a distinctive movement idiom which expressed the subject matter, and all the elements — dance, music, lighting, design — worked together to create a polyphonic but unified whole.

He spent his evenings in the studio with a selection of gramophone records, improvising, watching himself in the mirrors, searching for new shapes, new movements. The vocabulary of academic ballet was as fixed as tram tracks: legs turned out from the hips, spine locked solid, every movement contained and controlled. Alone in the studio he tore himself apart, turning his legs in, cracking his arms at the elbow, swinging, lunging, plunging, collapsing and falling. He strung some of these fragments into a sequence and tried to move inside the music. But he could see that it didn't really work. And he had no idea why.

He worked on alone for awhile, and some nights it felt like he was getting closer and other nights it didn't. He wished there was someone he could ask about it, but there was no one. Galina he could not approach until it was perfect (she would be satisfied with nothing less than perfection). Eventually he decided it would have to be Posy.

He hated having to ask. He felt as if it diminished him somehow. That he ought to just *know*. But he didn't know, and he wasn't willing to let it go. So he asked.

'When you make a ballet, how do you do it?'

Posy thought about it.

'I listen to the music,' she said finally, 'and think about how it makes me feel.'

This was no help at all.

He began to read everything he could find about Nijinsky. Vaslav Nijinsky exploded onto the world scene with the Ballets Russes in 1909, changing ballet irrevocably. Before Nijinsky, a male dancer was little more than a hat stand. After him, the male dancer became an equal partner to the ballerina. Nijinsky's technique, his stage presence, his power, his charisma, were given wings by the new choreography of Michel Fokine, blowing away for ever the sexless gentility of the old world. Nijinsky was mad and bad, sexy and dangerous. He created four amazing ballets — including one, *Le Sacre du Printemps*, which caused a riot. His career was vertiginously short: his four ballets were all completed by the time he was twenty-four. He was Diaghilev's lover, but then turned his back on him and married a woman, prompting his dismissal from the Ballets Russes. At thirty-two he was admitted to a mental institution, where he would spend the remainder of his life. There was something Teddy found sublime about this short, tragic life, so filled with genius, so abruptly cut off, so modern and so brief. (His madness seemed like a kind of death.) What a trajectory it had been: straight up and straight down, in only a dozen years, from heaven to hell.

He began to imagine a biographical ballet which would tell Nijinsky's story. He could use elements of Nijinsky's own ballets! He would dance the lead himself! It would be daring and innovative and completely modern! He started nosing out pieces of music. The composition grew and grew — at least in his imagination. He sketched costumes and wrote scenarios and devised and re-devised the cast list. He wondered if he could cast Galina as Diaghilev (wouldn't that be hilarious?).

Thirteen

The choreography eluded him. But the concept was enthralling.

He sat in on a rehearsal of one of Posy's ballets which was to be reprised for the new season. It was an ensemble piece and he and Galina did not appear in it. (Placed in the middle of the program, it gave them both a breather.) It was plotless, danced to a Mozart concerto, and although it gave an illusion of simplicity, the movement was as intricately patterned as a canon. The girls — exquisitely drilled as ever — moved in subtle and ever-changing formations, geometric yet liquid, in a series of movements which developed, he realised, out of a single sequence which was both simple and beautiful: a long, extended arabesque which reversed through a turn into another arabesque with an armline that swayed like the wind in branches. It was so simple and yet so perfect. It was academic, classical, but in a streamlined, purified way. There was nothing stiff and formal about it, although the girls' spines stayed as rigid as ever. He realised that Posy, apparently without effort, had developed a pure, clear voice of her own, which sat wholly within the framework of traditional ballet without being wedded to the past. It was beautiful. And he was furious with her.

It wasn't because she was a baby (although that was a part of it). It wasn't because he knew he had a serious rival (although that, too, was a part of it — a big part). It was because it was clearly so *effortless*. Because he knew that she *had* just gone into the studio and done what the music told her to do. Because for her there seemed to be no gap between intention and achievement.

He told himself that he was aiming much higher than she was, that he was trying to start a revolution, while she was just keeping things rolling along on their stately old path. But it didn't comfort him very much.

She became an itch that he could not quite manage to scratch. It had to be a trick, he thought. It couldn't be so easy for her, it just couldn't. She seemed like such a straightforward, clean-living, untutored, unthinking girl from the suburbs. She was cheery and good-natured. She liked sunbaking and ice-cream and her nose was always peeling. She did not appear to have a dark, tormented, tragic bone in her body. So where did it come from, this gift she had?

He found himself nosing around her, circling her. Other girls would have become flustered, or flirtatious; not her. She was like clear water, fathoms deep, unruffled, unvarying, shadowless. He tried to uncover what made her tick, but could not get close enough to make sense of her. He took her out, bought her drinks, plied her with questions. She was never evasive but still she slipped through his fingers. It was like going to sea in a sieve. He coaxed her back to his house for supper. She had not been there before and he saw her eyes widen as she took in the décor. He had taken some time on it and he was rather proud of the effect — luxurious but bohemian, a sumptuous clutter of books and music and *objets d'art*, the home of someone who loved beautiful things but didn't much care about dreary bourgeois notions of good taste.

'Nice place,' she remarked.

'Let me get you a drink,' he said suavely.

Thirteen

She perched on his shabby sofa and watched while he did his Man of the World routine at the drinks cabinet.

'I'm a bit tipsy,' she observed as he handed her a drink.

'What a delightful way to be,' he replied, sliding onto the couch beside her.

'Do you live here by yourself?' she asked, as he sipped his drink and stared at her.

'Of course.'

'Must be nice to have a place of your own. Mother and Father make the most fearful fuss about the hours I keep.'

'Why don't you move out then?'

'Oh, I couldn't. They'd be so upset.'

'How old are you, Posy?'

'Twenty-two.'

He smiled, and gazed at her. Her ice-cream-coloured skin was vivid with freckles and she seemed to be bursting out of her dun-coloured suit, which did not suit her at all. She had a tomboyish air of wilful disarray which sat a little incongruously with her chosen profession. Onstage she was as lacquered as every other little swan, but now she looked as if she'd arrived like Dorothy, on the wind. Or been dragged through a hedge backwards.

On an impulse he took her drink from her, parked it on the coffee table and briskly kissed her. Her lips against his were soft and startled, and she did not kiss him back. In the space of a breath she had planted a hand on his chest and pushed him off.

'What was that all about?'

'That, my dear, was what they call a kiss.'

She frowned at him. 'Don't talk like that.'

'Like what?'

'Like I'm some silly girl in a film. I'm not.'

He identified the look on her face. It was disappointment.

'Sorry, old thing. I thought you might like it.'

He wasn't sure what he'd expected, but it hadn't been this. He'd thought she might melt into his arms, or at the very least slap him. Either of those reactions he would have known how to deal with. But instead she was staring at him with those disconcertingly intelligent eyes, as if she had seen something in him that she didn't much like.

'You're not interested in me,' she said. 'I know it and you know it. So why did you kiss me?'

Not knowing what to say, he looked away and lit a cigarette.

'I thought we were friends,' she said, exasperated.

'And so we are.'

She was still looking at him with that curiously penetrating look. 'Well, don't do it again.'

After that, they *were* friends.

He would never underestimate her again.

❋ ❋ ❋

They had dinner together several times in the weeks following the auditions. He toyed with the idea of asking her to become his ballet mistress but couldn't quite bring himself to do it, although he couldn't have said why. They avoided reminiscences. But then one night, when they had had a little more Chianti to drink than usual, Posy said, 'She blames you, you know.'

It came out of the blue, but Teddy knew exactly who she was talking about. 'Galina? Why?'

Thirteen

'She thinks you tried to steal her company.'

'What gave her such a bizarre idea? Not that Galina was ever a stranger to bizarre ideas.'

'That's what John told her.'

'But it's not true.'

Posy shrugged. 'It's what she believes.'

He found himself unaccountably agitated by the thought that Galina still bore him ill will after all this time, not that he was particularly surprised by it. He had never met anyone who could bear a grudge with such commitment and venom.

'Are you still friends with her?'

'Oh no.'

'What happened?'

'She cut us all off when the company folded. I think she was embarrassed — the business with the money was all so awful, and she felt that she'd let us down. I was rather hurt, to tell you the truth. I thought our friendship was stronger than that. But when she married John, she turned her back on her old life. Became a card-carrying society matron.'

'*Galina?*'

'You know what she was like. Whatever she did, she had to be the best at it. When she was a dancer, she had to be the best dancer. If she was going to be a society wife, she was going to be the best at that, too. She threw herself into the role and turned into a completely different person. She never looked back.'

'How terribly sad.'

'She's very rich,' Posy said dismissively. 'Her house has been in *Belle*.'

'But she wanted to be Pavlova.'

Possibly it was the drink, but suddenly he wanted to cry. So they had humbled her in the end. Turned her from something extraordinary into something bourgeois and suburban.

Posy sipped her Chianti thoughtfully. 'What did happen between you and Galina?' she asked.

Teddy felt the hair prickle on the back of his neck. 'Why do you ask?'

'I always knew something had happened between you but I never knew what.'

'You wouldn't believe me if I told you,' Teddy said casually, but in a tone that deflected any further questions. To his relief, Posy did not pursue the matter.

Fourteen

MONEY — JOHN — THE SNOW QUEEN — CRISIS

Pavlova's company

In 1911 Pavlova left the Imperial Ballet and formed her own company. Pavlova was fortunate to have as her husband (although it was rumoured that he was not, officially speaking, her husband) Baron Victor Dandre, a man of great wealth and influence, who was responsible for organising and managing the company so that she was free to think only of her dancing. For such a company to come into existence, there must be two things: first, there must be an individual with a great artistic vision. Second, there must be someone behind the scenes, someone who is able to read the train timetables and who knows how fifty pieces of luggage can be transported cheaply, someone who can hire and fire and negotiate, someone who has money, or access to people with money. There is no artistry without money.

I meet John

As manager, principal choreographer and ballerina of the Koslova Ballet, I had to wear many hats and perform many tasks. It was one of my jobs to try and attract backers for my company. I was fortunate that my early successes as a teacher had given me access to the artistic community of Adelaide. Many of their daughters attended my school and some of them had graduated to become dancers in my company. So I was often invited to parties where the people with money congregated.

It was at one of these parties, early in 1947, that I first met John Black. He was pointed out to me as I arrived. He was, I was told, a widower — such a tragic story, his wife had been killed in a car accident, leaving him with a small daughter to bring up alone. He was thinking of sending his little girl along to ballet lessons and who better to give lessons than I? He was also, I was told, in the washing machine business. When I heard this I was not interested at all. A man who sells washing machines? Why should I be interested in a salesman? He doesn't *sell* them, I was told. He *makes* them — along with refrigerators and all the other conveniences of the modern home. He was not a rich man then — although he was doing well enough — but in the years to come he would become very wealthy indeed. (The 1950s were a very good time for white goods.) So we were introduced.

Fourteen

I found John to be a charming man, so dishy in his dinner suit. He had the suavity of an antipodean Cary Grant, although he was not sophisticated in the manner of the European men I knew. Adelaide breeds a certain kind of man who prides himself on his cosmopolitanism and has a patrician sort of interest in the arts. These men are not *passionate* about the arts: in this country, a man can only be passionate about sport, or perhaps racing. If anything else stirs his blood it is seen as evidence of homosexuality. But these men regard the arts as a Good Thing, rather like public parks or charitable organisations, and so they support them in any way they can. At that time John was an opera buff, and sometimes went to a classical music concert, but he had never attended the ballet.

We must remedy that, I said, and gave him an invitation to my next performance. He said he would be delighted to come and see me dance. I could not tell whether he was merely being polite or whether he would actually attend, but to my surprise and pleasure, he sent a card around to my dressing room after my very next performance, saying he had been in the audience and had enjoyed the show very much. He invited me to have supper with him and I accepted the invitation with great interest.

John was an instant convert. He wanted to know everything about me, about Russia and Paris, my company, my plans for the future. I talked to him of our forthcoming tour, of my choreographic ideals, my dream of building a great ballet company which would be the equal of any in Europe. John had similarly high hopes for the country of his birth. Why, he said, must we go through life assuming that the best of everything comes from Europe? America is a new country, just like us, and they do not allow themselves to be overshadowed by the achievements of the European past. They look only to the future, and so should we. How we talked! We outlasted the yawning waiters who eventually started to put the chairs up on the tables to make us leave. A bond was formed that night, but I do not think I realised how serious that bond would become until much later.

I received a phone call from John the very next day, inviting me to lunch. He said he had a proposal to make.

We ate lunch in the very best restaurant Adelaide had to offer. John had been greatly inspired by our talk and he was there, he said, to put his money where his mouth was. He was ready, in short, to put some money into funding my tour.

The only catch, he said with a smile, was that he would like it very much if I would consent, from time to time, to have dinner with him. As he was a charming man, this did not seem an arduous duty. So I consented.

I know that later, after I married him, it was whispered in certain circles that I had *set my cap* for John, that I had *artfully snared him*. In fact, the opposite was the case. I was not looking for a husband, then or at any other time. It was John, widowed over a year before, who was looking for a wife. I was not naïve — I could see that he was as charmed by me as I was by him. I was not above turning this to my own advantage if it meant that the work could proceed. But as far as I was concerned, there was never any ambiguity about our relationship. When I accepted his money, I was wearing my professional hat as manager of the Koslova Ballet. It was never

Fourteen

implied or suggested that I was also consenting to become his mistress. John was always the perfect gentleman towards me, and his professional dealings with the Koslova Ballet were entirely above reproach. He was my chief supporter and financial backer in those last glorious, terrible days, no less and no more. Our romantic entanglement did not begin until the ballet was no more. Anyone who suggests otherwise is defaming both myself and him.

Mr Wilkinson's proposal

Over the years I had developed a professional relationship with a man who owned a chain of theatres, Mr Wilkinson. People understood about theatres in those days, although even then they were being turned into picture palaces. Mr Wilkinson's chain was the most successful in the country and all the big acts played there. Not just the ballet, but plays from England and musical comedies and every kind of quality entertainment you could think of, even opera. There was an appetite then among all kinds of people, not just the rich, for live entertainment. Television killed it, in the end.

In the autumn of 1948 Mr Wilkinson asked me to come and see him to discuss our forthcoming tour. Teddy came with me to all my business meetings, for although in reality he had no role in the company other than *premier danseur*, he had agreed to stand in as my producer whenever we had to meet with bank managers, hotel managers, theatre managers and every other kind of manager that I was obliged to have dealings with. It made things so much easier if I could give the impression there was a man in charge — even if it was only Teddy, who could not have taken charge of the proverbial piss-up in a brewery. Teddy would dress up for these occasions in a terribly severe suit and a navy blue tie and become stodgy and pompous (this was how he imagined men of business spoke to each other). Over time, his performance became so exaggerated that I was forced to make him tone it down, as the contrast between his onstage and his business personae was so great that even the managers were beginning to find it odd.

Mr Wilkinson ran a very efficient operation — so efficient, in fact, that most of our previous dealings had been conducted quite satisfactorily by letter. So it was most unusual to be called in for a meeting with him. Filled with curiosity, Teddy and I went to the theatre to see him.

'What have you got for me?' Mr Wilkinson asked. 'What are you planning to put on?'

'It will be a double bill,' I told him. 'Two new ballets, one to be choreographed by Teddy, one to be choreographed by Posy. We feel that the time is right for such a thing.'

'New Australian works for an Australian public wanting to look forward, not back,' Teddy added.

I was tired of touring old *divertissements* from my days with the Ballets Russes, and my dancers were tired of it, and I felt sure that audiences were tired of it too. But Mr Wilkinson did not think so.

'It's risky,' he said. 'How about one new work mixed in with some old favourites? You could do your swan solo again, people love that one.'

To my shame, I had done a version of *Le Cygne* that Michel Fokine had made for Pavlova. I had seen it performed many

Fourteen

times in Paris, and with my prodigious memory I was able to recreate the choreography, although I had never danced it myself. Pavlova toured Australia twice in her long career and was an idol to audiences here. They all wanted to see *Le Cygne*. For them it was the essence of ballet and they would not go home happy unless they saw it. I could understand their feelings, and I was willing to do it if it pleased them. But I always felt like a fraud dancing her solo.

'The audience have seen me do it so many times, they could jump up onstage and do it with me,' I said.

'Well, what are these two new ballets about?' Mr Wilkinson asked. 'What are their subjects? Will they be popular?'

'Whether they will be popular I cannot say, but I can assure you they will be significant works of art. Forgive me, Mr Wilkinson, but why do you care what the works are about?'

'I have a proposition for you,' Mr Wilkinson said.

Mr Wilkinson explained that he was interested in putting some money into the Koslova Ballet. Instead of hiring his theatres to us, he would become our producer. He would give us his backing, spend money on promotion, help bring in guest stars from overseas. He thought that in time, if all went well and things turned out as he hoped, we might be able to have a real orchestra to accompany our performances, instead of pianists and gramophone records. There would be more money for costumes and beautiful sets, more money to pay the dancers. Mr Wilkinson made it sound like a dream come true and Teddy was very excited, but I was more cautious.

'And what would you expect of us in return?' I asked.

'Well,' said Mr Wilkinson, 'I'd expect a share of the profits.'

'Naturally.'

'And I'd want to have some say in what you were putting on.'

'I see.'

'Your company could be useful to me in other ways too — in operetta, for example, it's often nice to have a little ballet. Your dancers could do that sort of thing, couldn't they, as long as they weren't needed for a tour. It'd only be classy stuff, mind. I wouldn't get them tap-dancing or high-kicking. Leave that to the experts, eh?'

Mr Wilkinson winked at me. I was horrified.

'How on earth could you imagine we would be involved in any such thing?' I said. 'Doing dances for an *operetta*, whatever that may be. I am not a jobbing ballet mistress, my dancers are not hacks for hire.'

'Well, we could sort all that out later,' Mr Wilkinson said soothingly. 'So anyway, what do you think? Would you be interested in principle?'

'Yes, certainly, in principle,' Teddy said. 'I'm sure we can sort out all these other little details. Thank you, Mr Wilkinson, it's a very generous offer, and I can assure you, you won't regret it.'

'Tell me, Mr Wilkinson,' I interrupted. 'What about our double bill?'

Mr Wilkinson rubbed unhappily at his neck. 'I'd have to say, Miss Koslova, that I wouldn't be too happy about that at all. Two new works — it's a risky proposition, very risky indeed.'

'If you were our producer, would you let us put on a double bill?'

Fourteen

'It would depend. Obviously there'd need to be some detailed consultation ...'

'Yes or no, Mr Wilkinson.'

He rubbed at his neck again. 'No,' he admitted.

'Well, in that case there is nothing more to say.'

Mr Wilkinson looked at Teddy for help. 'There's no need to be so hasty about this,' he said. 'I'm sure you and I can find a solution to this. It really will be the best thing for everyone.'

Teddy looked at me beseechingly, but I was not budging.

'Once Miss Koslova's made up her mind there's not much I can do,' Teddy said regretfully. 'Temperament, you know.'

'Ah,' Mr Wilkinson said, nodding knowledgeably.

Teddy gave me a scolding when we left the office.

'Why did you do that?' he said. 'If you'd taken the money all our problems would be over.'

'He's a theatre-owner. He owns *buildings*. What does he know about art?'

'He must know something, since he's rich and we're broke.'

I shrugged this off. 'Koslova Ballet is *my* ballet,' I said, 'and while it is my ballet, I make the decisions. I will not have a man who owns buildings telling me what to put in my seasons.'

'Would it kill you to compromise?' Teddy said, exasperated.

'Once you compromise,' I said haughtily, 'what is the point in continuing?'

The truth about the double bill

What Teddy did not seem to realise was that if anyone's ballet were to be dropped from the program, it was unlikely to be Posy's. Her works had almost universally found favour with critics and audiences alike. It was Teddy's ballets which were rather more shaky, and it was Teddy I was protecting. If Mr Wilkinson had his way, there would have been no more ballets by Edward Larwood. He didn't have to say it — I knew what he meant. But Teddy was such an egotist he would not allow himself to see the truth. He would always laugh off his failures, saying he was too radical for the plebs who wrote for the newspapers, they didn't understand him, great artists are never appreciated in their own lifetime, and so on and so forth. I did not want to crush him, so I did not argue with him. And besides, I had a kind of faith in him. Even after two years of watching him putting up slapdash work as if it was finished, I still hoped that in time he would knuckle under, he would really put his heart and soul into a work, and he would actually manage to achieve something. He needed a breakthrough. This tour, the 1948 tour, was his chance to succeed — and, as it turned out, it would be his last chance.

The Snow Queen (2)

I had decided to create a ballet based upon the story of 'The Snow Queen'. For those who are unfamiliar with the story, it goes something like this.

The Snow Queen had a magic mirror. One day two of her naughty attendants stole the mirror and accidentally broke it. Shards of the magic mirror flew out across the world, lodging in the hearts of unsuspecting people and turning their hearts to ice, so that they became cold and hard and lost all affection for their friends and family. In a certain village lived two children, a girl called Gerda and a boy called Kay. They lived next door to

Fourteen

each other and were the best of friends. Gerda's grandmother had given her a rose bush, and every day she and Kay would tend the rose bush together. One day they were out playing in the snow when Kay suddenly cried out in pain. He had been struck in the eye by a shard of the magic mirror. The pain soon passed, but Kay underwent a swift and subtle change. His heart grew cold and he forgot his former affection for Gerda. He ran off to the edge of town, where the naughty boys liked to play, taking his little sledge with him. He had not been there very long when he saw a great sleigh drawn by two strong white horses. 'That sleigh will give me a good ride,' he thought and so he hooked his little sledge to the back of it. When the sleigh took off, it went so fast that Kay felt as if he was flying. Faster and faster it went, until Kay was quite lost and starting to become frightened. 'Stop, stop!' he cried. Eventually the sleigh did stop and the driver turned to look at him.

'Don't be afraid,' he said, and Kay realised the driver was not a man but a woman, a very tall and beautiful woman. And then he realised that the furs she was wearing were not furs at all but robes of ice. She was the Snow Queen.

'Do not be afraid,' she said again. 'Come and ride with me.'

And then she gave him a kiss, and on the instant Kay forgot everything: his home, his family, even Gerda and the rose bush. His heart, with the shard of the magic mirror in it, turned entirely to ice. He was under the Snow Queen's spell and they drove off together to her palace in the north.

Gerda knew nothing of the spell which had been placed upon Kay and so she set out to find him. For days she walked, looking everywhere for him, but she could find no sign of him.

Finally she came to a house where a kind old lady lived. The lady asked her in and gave her food to eat and let her rest her tired feet. But Gerda did not realise that the woman was a witch and the food she had been given was enchanted. The old lady, who longed for a daughter of her own, had cast a spell on her that made her forget everything: Kay, her journey, even her own name. For a time Gerda lived very happily with the witch. But then one day she happened to see a rose blooming and it reminded her of the rose bush she had left at home, and at once all her memories came flooding back. 'I must get on!' Gerda cried. 'I have lost so much time already!' So she said goodbye to the witch and went on.

When she had been walking many days she met with a great crow, who asked her where she was going. When she told the crow her story, the crow said he had seen a young boy just like Kay in the palace of the princess. The princess, who was very clever but very lonely, had encountered a young boy wandering lost upon the road and she had taken him back to the palace to live with her. When Gerda heard this she was very excited and she went to the palace straight away. But when at last she was allowed into the throne room, she discovered that the boy, although he resembled Kay, was not Kay, and so she shed many a tear. The princess, taking pity on her, offered to give her a horse and a carriage so that she might continue her search. Gerda thanked the princess gratefully and went on her way.

She had not been travelling long when she was held up by a band of robbers, who stole her horse and her carriage and the pretty clothes the princess had given her, and she was lucky that they did not cut her throat for good measure. But she begged

Fourteen

and pleaded with them, and told them her sad story, and the robber chief's daughter took pity on her.

'I cannot give you back your horse and carriage,' she said, 'but perhaps this reindeer will be able to help you. He is old and very wise.'

The reindeer said he had heard a rumour that the Snow Queen had passed through on her way to the north and that she had a boy with her. 'I can take you to the north,' said the reindeer, 'as that is my childhood home.'

So the reindeer took Gerda upon his back and together they went bounding across the snowy fields until they came to the house of an old, old woman.

'Can you tell us the way to the Snow Queen's palace?' asked the reindeer.

'You must go to the house of my sister in Finland,' said the old woman. 'She will be able to help you.' So she wrote a message to her sister on a piece of dried cod and sent them on their way.

When they reached the house of the old Finnish woman, Gerda was surprised to see nothing but a chimney jutting out of the snow.

'It is so cold here that she lives inside a chimney,' said the reindeer. 'It is the best way to keep warm.'

So they went inside the chimney-house and handed the old woman the message written on the piece of dried cod. The old Finnish woman told them they were very near to the Snow Queen's palace and that Kay was certainly there. Gerda was frightened about meeting the queen, but the old woman told her not to be afraid.

'The Snow Queen is away on her travels,' she said, 'and your own gentle goodness is all the power you will need to defeat her.'

So the reindeer took Gerda to the very gates of the Snow Queen's palace, which were guarded by a holly tree. 'I can take you no further,' said the reindeer. 'You must go in there alone.'

So Gerda went in, trembling with fear. The palace was guarded by whirling snowflakes which twisted and writhed and turned themselves into terrifying shapes: lions and tigers and snakes and monsters. But they were only snowflakes, after all, and when Gerda pushed through them they blew apart. The Snow Queen's palace was enormous, made entirely of glistening blue ice. As she walked through the corridors her feet threatened to slip out from under her, and everywhere she went the only sound was the drip, drip of water and the crack, crack of ice creaking and groaning. At last she came to the Snow Queen's throne room and there she found Kay, sitting on a little seat beside the Snow Queen's throne. He was quite stunned and stupefied with cold and his hands and lips were blue. Gerda ran up to him and threw her arms about him and her warm, salty tears began to flow. As her tears fell upon his face, the splinter of mirror was washed away and his heart began to thaw.

'Gerda?' he said. 'What are you doing here?'

'I have come to take you home,' said Gerda.

'The Snow Queen has me under a spell,' said Kay. 'I cannot leave the palace until I have turned these letters into a word.'

Kay showed her a collection of letters made of ice and together they moved the letters around until they made a word. And the word was ETERNITY. The spell was broken and all of a sudden they found themselves standing once more in the open air beside the holly bush, where the reindeer was waiting to take them home. And when at last they returned to their village, they found their little rose bush had burst into bloom, and Gerda wore one of the blooms in her hair when she married Kay, and the two of them lived happily ever after.

Making a ballet

There were many things that appealed to me about this story. The tale required some streamlining (there were far too many old ladies in it), but I decided to show it to Posy and see what she could do with it.

Posy usually came up with her own ideas, but she had from time to time taken my suggestions and developed choreography around them. I showed her my scenario for the ballet and loaned her a gramophone record (I had selected some suitable music) so that she might listen to it and think about it. She rang me the next day in a state of high excitement.

'I have some ideas,' she said, 'but there's something I have to ask you. How would you feel about dancing the role of the Snow Queen instead of Gerda?'

'I never intended anything else,' I said.

Making a ballet (2)

This was the outline that I gave her.

Prologue: The Snow Queen gazes into her magic mirror. She sees in it an image of Kay. She leaves her castle and her goblin attendants make mischief with the mirror. It shatters and the goblins run away in terror.

Scene 1: A happy village scene. Gerda, Kay and the village boys and girls dance around the rose bush. They are happy and in love. Their celebration is interrupted when Kay is struck by a piece of the magic mirror. He cries out in pain, but then his heart turns slowly to ice. He cruelly repudiates Gerda and runs from her. The girl is broken-hearted. The goblins from the prologue emerge from their hiding place and are well pleased with their mischief.

Scene 2: Kay runs to another part of the forest, where he sees the Snow Queen alight from her sleigh. They dance a duet and, at the end of it, Kay gets into the sleigh and rides away, just as Gerda comes looking for him.

Scene 3: Gerda sets out on her journey. She meets the crow, who sends her to the palace. The court dance, then Gerda meets the princess and her consort, who give her a carriage. She is threatened by the robbers, who do a threatening dance. Then the robber's daughter introduces her to the reindeer, who takes her to the palace of the Snow Queen.

Scene 4: The snowflakes dance, and then Gerda goes into the palace where she discovers Kay. Her tears melt his frozen heart and they dance a joyous duet before fleeing the palace of the Snow Queen. The Snow Queen returns to find herself alone and dances a sad solo.

Scene 5: The happy couple return to their village, where they celebrate their love among the dancing villagers.

Rehearsals

We began to prepare for our forthcoming tour. Company class was held every morning from nine until ten, and then rehearsals began: *The Snow Queen* from ten until one, Teddy's as-yet-

Fourteen

untitled ballet from two until five. Posy was always very organised in her approach and her rehearsals went smoothly. The ballet took shape quickly and showed every sign of being a masterpiece. I was not in Teddy's ballet, so I had no idea how his work was proceeding. He liked to keep his creative process very private, and I did not wish to intrude so I asked no questions. He had assembled a small cast of dancers which did not overlap with mine and so I heard nothing.

One morning, Teddy did not turn up as scheduled for a rehearsal of *The Snow Queen*. As he was not known for his punctuality, I thought nothing of it, but when a full hour had elapsed and there was still no sign of him, I rang his house. There was no answer. We carried on without him, but I began to worry, and when Teddy did not appear for his own rehearsal that afternoon, I had the first inkling that something might be wrong. That evening I went around to his house. It was in darkness, locked and silent. There was clearly no one there. I appealed to the members of the company — had any of them heard from Teddy, did they have some clue as to his whereabouts? But no one knew anything.

I was frantic. Had something happened to him? Could he have been the victim of foul play? And if not, where was he? As the days passed, certain facts came to light. Work on his ballet had not been going well; in fact, it had gone very badly. He had made numerous false starts, changing his mind about what he wanted every day. The day before he disappeared, he had had a tantrum in the rehearsal room and thrown all his dancers out in disgust. Why had nobody seen fit to inform me of this, I asked. The dancers said they had been under strict instructions not to tell.

It began to seem very likely that Teddy had simply run away.

I began to rehearse a set of our old *divertissements* to fill out the program. Even if Teddy came back, it seemed impossible that he could complete any sort of ballet in time. I was furious. How could he be so unprofessional? But I also felt compassion for him. It is very difficult for such a personality to face the prospect of failure.

John makes a proposal

John and I had been seeing each other for the occasional dinner or supper over the past year, and we had become fast friends. When an invitation came in the midst of all my troubles I jumped at the chance. A relaxing evening out with a good friend sounded like just what I needed. But when John arrived to collect me, all spruced up in his Sunday best, I sensed that this would be no ordinary dinner. When we reached the restaurant — it was quiet, elegant, intimate; in fact, *very romantic* — John insisted on the best bottle of champagne the restaurant had to offer.

'What are we celebrating?' I asked.

'Do we need a reason?' he replied.

The champagne was excellent and it came with caviar in the Russian style, and we ate oysters and lobster until we were practically sick. Then, in the traditional lull between dinner and dessert, it came.

'You must know,' John said, 'how I feel about you.'

'I hope that we are very good friends,' I replied.

'Of course we are,' said John. 'But I'd like us to be something more than that.'

Fourteen

He reached into his pocket then and took out a small velvet box. Inside was a ring with a diamond large enough to dazzle a Romanov.

'Will you marry me?' he asked.

Although I had known there was something in the air, I was still surprised by his proposal.

'Oh John,' I think I said, 'I don't know what to say.'

'How about yes,' he said, and we both laughed.

I was flattered, and also very tempted. John was the most charming and attractive man I had met in some time and I knew he would make a good husband. And yet I knew that the timing was not right.

So I asked him if I could have some time to think about it, and he said of course, and we had a lovely dessert of *îles flottantes*, coffee and brandy, and he took me home.

Marriage and the dancer

When a girl takes up a career as a ballet dancer she must make many sacrifices. First among these is her romantic life.

Ballet is a profession for single girls. There are very few working dancers who are also married women. Ballet is such a hard taskmaster that there is not room in a dancer's life for both a husband and a career. To try and do both is like being unfaithful. Either the career or the husband will end up neglected, and for the true artist, this is an intolerable state of affairs.

From an early age I knew that dancing was my one true love, and I never did meet anyone who tempted me to leave the stage while I was at the height of my career. In that way, I was lucky. I knew many other girls who agonised long and hard about giving up their careers for the men they loved. It is not an easy thing, giving up the life of the stage. There is something about the admiration of an audience, the experience of seeing your name in the newspapers, being recognised upon the street, that is deeply satisfying in a way that the love of just one man can never be.

My answer

I must confess that my mind was not really focused on rehearsal the day after John proposed. Should I say yes? Should I say no? I could not make up my mind. I believed then (and I believe now) that when a woman marries, she should give up her single life and devote herself to her family. John would never force me to give up my career, but it would be impossible for me to run the company, take rehearsals every day, dance every night and go away on tour, while at the same time taking care of his house, looking after his little girl and being a proper wife to him. The decision caused me a great deal of heartache, for I knew that John truly loved me and would make me a good husband; but in the end I realised that I could not marry him. There was so much that I still wanted to do and I was not ready to give it up. I cared for him, but I loved my company more.

John took it very well, although he was disappointed.

'I hope we can still be friends,' he said.

'I hope so too,' I said.

He assured me that of course he would not think of taking his money out of the company. He had promised to back me, no strings attached, and so the tour would go ahead as planned.

Fourteen

I was very relieved to hear this, but, as I say, his behaviour in all things was perfectly gentlemanly.

Teddy returns

A week after he disappeared, Teddy turned up again as if nothing had happened. When I quizzed him about where he had been, he was insouciant.

'I had to take some time off to gather my thoughts,' he said.

I was very angry with him. I told him I knew he had made no headway with his ballet. I told him he was cowardly and unprofessional. I told him I had pulled his ballet from the program and replaced it with *divertissements*. I told him he would never have another opportunity to choreograph again if this was the way he was going to behave. He snapped back that if I hadn't been so incredibly demanding and taken up all his time with rehearsals for Posy's ballet then he would have had enough time and energy to concentrate on his own. I told him he was simply lazy and looking for excuses. He said that he was not lazy but he wasn't a robot, and he bet that he *could* still come up with a ballet in time. I told him it could not be done. He said, try me. I said, all right, but I would continue to rehearse the *divertissements* just in case. He accused me of having no faith in him. I told him seeing was believing. He said he couldn't make a new ballet while he was needed for rehearsals for my ballet. I told him the understudy would go on in his place. He said that suited him just fine.

So I started training the understudy — a delightful young man, but he lacked Teddy's dramatic abilities — and Teddy disappeared into the studio with his chosen handful of dancers. Again, all was secrecy: I was not permitted to know what was going on in that room. In my innocence, I still hoped that he might come up with something, for I did wish to see him succeed, even though I was angry with him. He had a deadline of one week — after that, it would be impossible for sets and costumes to be made, and the posters and programs had to be at the printers. There was much whispering around the corridors — would he make it?

On the day of the deadline, Teddy came to see me. 'My ballet is ready,' he said.

'When can I see it?' I asked.

'I have called a full company rehearsal for four o'clock this afternoon. I will present my ballet then.'

He was very high-handed in his manner — as he had been since he returned from his mystery trip — but nothing alerted me as to what was to follow.

The Lodger

Scene 1: A demobbed soldier returns from the war. He is seeking lodgings. He meets a pretty girl and he discovers there is a room in her house to let. He takes the room, and the girl and the soldier dance a duet. They are interrupted by the girl's mother who shoos the girl away.

Scene 2: The soldier sits in his room polishing his shoes. The mother comes in with a jug of water. She puts it down but she doesn't leave. She too is attracted to the soldier, even though she is old and grotesque. She attempts to seduce him, to the soldier's dismay. After a series of increasingly acrobatic attempts to ensnare him, she takes a spectacular pratfall off a wardrobe and breaks her leg.

Fourteen

Scene 3: The mother, with her leg in plaster, sulks in a bath chair, while the soldier seduces the daughter behind her back. He offers her a ring and they smuggle in a priest. The mother tries to chase the priest away, but ends up sailing off into the wings to the sound of an enormous crash. Boy and girl are wed and dance a joyful duet.

The Lodger (2)

In all my years I had never known such a betrayal. That he should parody me so cruelly, I who had given him every opportunity! His ballet, which was raucous and ugly, was nothing but a sadistic and heartless satire on my own work. It was intended to hurt, and it did hurt. Teddy always had a mischievous streak — he enjoyed playing pranks on people, and his sense of humour could be cruel — but I had never known him to be quite so vicious. To this day I do not know what I did to deserve such treatment.

When the performance was over, I felt all eyes turn towards me. Everyone had turned out for Teddy's presentation: the dancers, the set designer, the wardrobe lady, the stage manager. He had held me up to ridicule in front of the entire company.

Teddy turned to me with a look of scarcely concealed triumph.

'Well?' he said. 'What do you think?'

It is a sign of my great self-control that I did not pick up my chair and break it over his head.

'It has a certain charm,' I said graciously. 'And the duet between the two young lovers in the first scene is attractive. But as for the rest of it, well ... comedy is so difficult to handle in ballet, isn't it?'

His expression turned ugly.

'They laughed,' he said, pointing to the dancers.

'Yes,' I said, 'there is always an audience for low, vulgar humour. But we are a ballet company, not a vaudeville revue. It's all a question of tone, you see. I like a comical ballet as well as the next person. But I can't abide grotesquerie onstage. I don't like ugliness.'

'If the world is full of ugly things, don't you think it's our duty as artists to represent them?' he suggested nastily.

'No, I do not,' I said. 'People come to see us to escape from ugliness, not to wallow in it. I am very sorry, Teddy, but I cannot include your ballet in the program.'

'Is that so?' said Teddy. 'Then I quit.'

Crisis meeting

Teddy had threatened to quit before. He had threatened to quit because I made him come to company class at nine o'clock in the morning. He had threatened to quit because he didn't like his costume (I will *not* be seen onstage in green!). He had threatened to quit because he didn't like a hotel room in Brisbane. He had threatened to quit over minor casting choices (I'm not dancing with Miss X — she's terribly plain and her overbite is so enormous I'm afraid she's going to leave toothmarks all over me!). He had threatened to quit because there were not enough flowers in his dressing room, or his notices in the newspapers were not fawning enough (That's it! I'm going back to London! At least they appreciate real artistry over there!). He had threatened to quit over the smallest slight, real or imagined, but the threats had never come to anything. He

Fourteen

had never set me up for ridicule, or flouted my authority, or stormed out on me in front of a room full of people. This was like nothing he had ever done before.

I asked John to talk to him on my behalf. I could not trust myself to do it — I was too angry. But I still hoped that something could be done.

John went and talked to Teddy. When he came back he was very grave.

'It's serious,' he said.

'Why? What does he want?'

'He wants to be co-director of the company.'

I was outraged. 'It is *my* company, *mine*!'

'He says you asked him to be co-director, but you never listen to anything he says and veto all his decisions.'

'He knew perfectly well when I asked him to be co-director that it was only for show.'

'Did you put anything in writing?'

'No, of course not.'

'Well, it looks like he's changed his mind. He wants his new ballet back on the program, and from now on he wants an equal say in the running of the company.'

'Or what?'

'He's quitting, effective immediately.'

'He can't do that.'

'Is he under contract?'

'We had an agreement.'

'But there's nothing in writing?'

'No.'

John sighed. 'You should have got yourself a lawyer, Galina.'

'I have a lawyer. But that is for dealings with theatre managers and suppliers and so forth. Not for friends.'

'He's an employee as well as a friend.'

'I could not ask him to sign a contract. It would be rude.'

'It would have saved you a lot of trouble.'

'Well,' I said, 'what am I going to do about him?'

'You could put his ballet back on the program.'

'Impossible. The subject matter is vulgar, coarse and inappropriate, and the choreography is rushed and substandard. Even if the material were of an acceptable standard — which it is not — the two ballets cannot be performed side by side on the same program. It would be too ridiculous.'

'Why?'

'Teddy's ballet is a deliberate parody of *The Snow Queen*. I will not allow him to hold me or my dancers up to ridicule.'

'I don't suppose there's any point suggesting you give him more responsibility within the company?'

'Absolutely not! How can you even ask such a thing?'

John gave me a little smile. 'That's what I thought you'd say, but I had to be sure. Leave it with me. I'll handle it.'

I don't know what I would have done if I had not had John to help me. Teddy had turned on me in such a baffling and bewildering way that I did not know what else to do. That this challenge should come from Teddy of all people; Teddy, who had been such a dear friend to me in former days. It was all too puzzling and hurtful.

Meanwhile, our tour hung in the balance. As I think I have mentioned, our financial margins were extremely tight, and the situation at this late stage was grave. We had already spent money

Fourteen

on sets and costumes, hire of rehearsal rooms, wages for the pianist and dancers, travel bookings for dancers and equipment. We had costs to recoup and very little money in reserve. It was too late to back out now. We had to tour, no matter what.

John went to talk to Teddy once again. The situation had not improved. In fact it had deteriorated.

'He's not budging,' John said. 'Unless you're willing to make him co-artistic director, he's leaving.'

'Why is he doing this?' I said, exasperated.

'He's an egomaniac,' said John. 'It's as simple as that. He wants everything you've got, he thinks he deserves it.'

'I worked long and hard for what I've got,' I cried.

'He doesn't see it that way. He thinks you're jealous of his talent. He thinks you're trying to hold him back.'

'But that's not true! I have done everything humanly possible to encourage that man.'

'That's not the way he sees it,' John said.

'To hell with him then,' I said.

Teddy leaves

It was the end for me and Teddy. John conveyed my decision to him and asked him if he would consider staying on as *premier danseur*; but he was too proud. Through John, Teddy let me know that he would rather die than set foot on a stage with me ever again. So a partnership that had lasted two years came to an abrupt and permanent end. The next thing I heard, he had booked a passage back to London. I did not see him before he left, so that terrible day in the rehearsal room, when he presented his ballet *The Lodger,* was the last time I ever saw him face to face.

Fifteen

LAST TOUR — DEBT — WINDING UP OF COMPANY

Our last tour

It is painful for me to recall the details of that last tour. Teddy's departure hurt us for ticket sales were bad. Morale, too, was not all it might have been. Borovansky was at that stage preparing for a tour and my dancers started slinking off like rats from a sinking ship to join him. I gave my all, as I always did, but I must admit that without Teddy as Kay, *The Snow Queen* never again worked as well as it had in the rehearsal room, and we were unlucky that a foreign company with foreign stars had been on the same circuit only a few months before, eating into our potential audience. Our program received mixed reviews. In Adelaide we got nothing but praise and *The Snow Queen* was described as 'nothing short of a triumph'. The critic said of me: 'Miss Koslova dances with the exquisite artistry we have come to expect of her, performing the role of the Snow Queen with an expressiveness and pathos which is truly memorable.' Brisbane, too, was kind. The Melbourne critic was less enthusiastic about the ballet, but grudgingly admitted it was danced well. The Sydney critic ignored *The Snow Queen* completely to complain about the other part of the program, describing it as 'a tired and too-familiar program of *divertissements* which resembles nothing so much as yesterday's leftovers warmed up'. This I found the most insulting part of all. Had he arrived late? Hadn't he seen *The Snow Queen*? It seemed deeply unfair that he should so misrepresent us. I wrote a letter to the newspaper but I did not receive a reply. Nor was my letter printed on the Letters to the Editor page. We had hoped to make our money in Sydney, but the loss of Teddy, combined with the bad notices, sank us. We danced to half-empty houses, and the New Zealand leg of our tour was cancelled.

Pavlova's death

Anna Pavlova was famous for the purity and spirituality of her dancing, but she was also famous for her hard work. Such was her dedication to her audience that she toured constantly, appearing in every single performance her company gave. In her last tour of Australia, in 1929, her company gave 120 performances and she appeared in all of them. Not content with this, she also worked tirelessly to perfect her art, pushing herself twice as hard as the rest of her dancers. She was always the first to arrive at the theatre in the morning, and she would

Fifteen

often stay behind after a performance, practising alone until late into the night. She was about to embark on yet another tour when pneumonia took her life in 1931. She was fifty, and she had danced right up until the end.

Last days

When the tour ended, the company was in debt. I wanted to make sure that the dancers were paid — I did not want them to suffer for my misfortunes. But that left us with many creditors and no way of paying them.

One of them was Mr Wilkinson, who had offered to become my producer before the tour began. I had rejected him then, but I was not so proud now with ruin staring me in the face. So I went to see him.

Mr Wilkinson was as kind to me as ever, but he soon dashed my hopes.

'I'm sorry, Miss Koslova, but you should have been a bit quicker off the mark,' he said. 'The offer's no longer on the table.'

'But why not?' I asked.

'I can read a box office receipt as well as you can,' he said. 'I know how your last tour went.'

'That was unfortunate,' I said, 'but we were beset with many difficulties. Our next tour will be much more successful.'

'Maybe if you can get Mr Larwood back,' said Mr Wilkinson. 'But without him, I don't reckon you've got a hope.'

'Why not?'

'It was your partnership that people came to see. When the two of you got up onstage together sparks flew. Star quality, that's what it was.'

'I am still here, am I not?'

'Don't get me wrong — you're a star in your own right. But that kid you got as a replacement can't hold a candle to Mr Larwood. He's a hole in the stage.'

'He is young, inexperienced. I will find someone else.'

'I'm afraid the whole question's academic now anyway.'

'What do you mean?'

'I already told you, the offer's no longer on the table. After you turned me down the first time I thought you were serious, so I went looking elsewhere. I've already signed a contract with another ballet company.'

'Which other ballet company?'

'You'll hear soon enough. So you see, there really is no point in continuing this conversation. I'm very sorry I wasn't able to help you out, Miss Koslova. You should have come and seen me earlier.'

This other company had been promised exclusive use of Mr Wilkinson's theatres, so even if I was able to mount another tour, I would no longer be able to hire the best venues. Sydney had always had a chronic shortage of good theatres and Mr Wilkinson's theatre was really the only one I could consider using. If you couldn't get decent houses in Sydney, there was little point in touring at all. It was a terrible blow to my hopes.

I went to John and asked him for help. I knew he had already lost all the money he had put into the company, but I hoped that there might be something more he could do. He told me he was having some cash-flow problems but as soon as they were sorted out he would do whatever he could.

Fifteen

Our debts were too pressing, however, and I could not wait. I decided that in order to raise money we would sell all of our sets and costumes. John did not want me to do this, but I argued that it was costing us money to store them and we could always replace them in the future. Against his advice, I went ahead with the sale. (I did keep a few of my own costumes as mementoes — I was not so unsentimental that I could bear to part with everything.) Our sets and properties were not substantial — as a touring company, I could never afford anything so large it was difficult to transport — but I had high hopes for our costumes. They had been well designed and beautifully made and always attracted favourable notices. I was sure that this sale would raise a respectable sum of money. Alas, it was not to be. Although I had done my best to interest other professional companies, the only people who turned up were from amateur theatricals, church groups, little dancing schools, costume hire shops. They were there because they smelt a bargain, and in the end everything went for a song, leaving my debts virtually intact.

I went to John and confessed all. He was still in some financial difficulties, but he promised that he would speak to my remaining creditors. To this day, I don't know what arrangements were made, but eventually the debts were settled.

My company was dead. Our funds were all gone, our sets, our costumes. My backer was broke and my dancers had vanished — either to Borovansky's new company or to their old jobs as postmen and shopgirls. All I had left was my school — rented rooms — and my girls. It did not seem like much to show for eight years of struggle. I contemplated giving it all up and taking a passage for Paris, but the truth is I was broke and I had nothing left to sell. For the first time in my life, I felt completely helpless and alone. My dreams were in ruins, but, worse, I felt old. I had started from scratch in 1920 and again in 1940. But now it was 1948 and I could not do it a third time. Friends suggested I should give a benefit performance, as we had done at the start of the war when we first arrived in Adelaide, but after the many humiliations of the tour, I could not face the thought of appearing on a stage. I just wanted to put ballet behind me for ever.

John was once again my saviour. Three months after the last of my debts were paid, John and I were married.

❉ ❉ ❉

I could carry on writing about my life, my second life as an Australian wife, but I think it is time to stop. Before my marriage, my life was conducted in the public eye, before an audience; what followed was private and I do not think John would appreciate me writing about it.

Perhaps I will simply end by saying this: we all lived happily ever after.

Sixteen

What is there to say about my life after dance? What can anyone say? Time is rarely kind to dancers. I sometimes feel it would be better to shoot us, like racehorses, rather than let us retire. I think about my father, who retired on a pension from the Imperial Ballet. He thought his future was secure and then the revolution came along and swept it all away — the Imperial Ballet, the pensions, the past. All that work and he was left with nothing, no pension, no livelihood, no savings. His life all behind him. My parents left Petersburg in 1922 and I did not hear from them again. So much waste, on such a grand scale. I think of Pavlova, who wore a new pair of shoes for every performance she gave, and the huge pile of discarded satin shoes she must have left behind, broken-backed, scuffed and dirty from the stage. I think of my idol, Kschessinska, her beautiful house laid waste by Bolsheviks. When I was young,

I thought the Imperial Ballet would live for ever, that the art we made would be handed down through the generations as a treasure to be nurtured. I thought the name of Kschessinska would be immortal. She was the brightest star who had ever lived, the ornament of the Russian stage, a supreme artist, a legendary figure. But who remembers her now? Who remembers her dancing, the dancing that made her famous? There are photographs of her but they do not do justice to her living presence, the unique vibration of her charisma, that ineffable quality which drew your eye as soon as she appeared on the stage. I could describe her qualities all day, but for anyone who has not seen it for themselves, the descriptions are meaningless. They cannot convey the beauty of her art. When I and the others like me who remember her are all dead, there will be no living trace of Kschessinska remaining upon the earth, apart from a few cold relics. Her unique qualities will have vanished for ever.

And what of Pavlova? She was caught on film, true; but those old flickering images, jerky and jumpy, can only convey a sense of what we have lost. It is her shade that we are watching, not the true Pavlova, the flesh and blood Pavlova. We cannot ever hope to recapture her, because she is trapped, like all of us, in her time. Pavlova was the greatest ballerina of her day — some would say the greatest ballerina the world has ever known. But if you put her next to one of today's ballerinas, she would seem like nothing at all. Her artistry was of its time. Her technique, such as it was, was also of its time. Next to a modern ballerina she would look feeble, and sentimental, and weak, and (greatest of modern sins) *fat*. Her beauty does not

Sixteen

speak to us, nor does her expressiveness, her tenderness, her simplicity. To truly understand what made her great, it is necessary to have seen her at her peak, and to have seen audiences respond to her. Her art is inseparable from the moment in which it flourished; to compare it with the present is an act of heartless violence.

When I was young, I dreamed that one day I would make my mark upon the world, that I would do something that would fix me in history, so that I would never be forgotten. I suppose every child imagines this. I thought I would make my mark through art, by becoming a great ballerina. Later on, when I was perhaps old enough to know better, I thought that I would make it through my company. Even if my dancing was forgotten, I reasoned, my company would survive. How foolish I was! If the Imperial Ballet could not withstand the forces of history, why should I think my little company should be any different? Perhaps I imagined the winds of history blew less ferociously in this calm little backwater at the bottom of the world. But no; they blow just as strongly here as they do everywhere else.

But my memoir is written. That is something, I suppose. A ballet disappears in the moment that it comes into being, but a book is solid and permanent and real. The words are affixed firmly to the page and can be copied and copied again so they can never be lost. A ballet dancer is nothing but a match-flare in a hurricane, but a book anchors you to the ground, anchors you to history. It is not enough, but it is something.

❋ ❋ ❋

I have lunch with my step-daughter, Gwendolyn. Today she is wearing a badge saying 'Sisterhood is powerful'. As she is an only child I do not understand this, so I ask her what it means.

'It means what it says,' she says.

'You do not have a sister,' I point out.

'It means sisterhood in the political sense,' she says huffily, 'like the brotherhood of man.'

'People will think you're turning into a women's libber if you go round wearing things like that,' I warn her.

'People would be right,' she says.

I don't know what's come over Gwendolyn lately. I cannot put a foot right with her, she is always angry with me. John says it is because she is unhappy. (She has recently left her husband.) I think it is because she has new women's libber friends from university, dykes and man-haters, who are filling her head with funny ideas. Gwendolyn has stopped wearing make-up and gets around in terrible dungarees. I have even seen her out in public in a T-shirt with no bra underneath — a woman of thirty, with young children! It was *repellent*.

'Dad says you've written your memoirs,' Gwendolyn says.

'Yes I have,' I tell her. 'It was very difficult.'

'Will you try and publish them?'

'Of course,' I say. 'Why would I have written them otherwise?'

Gwendolyn eats for a while in silence then says shyly, 'I have a friend who might be interested in looking at them.'

I am surprised and touched. 'Who is he?'

'She,' corrects Gwendolyn. 'She's part of a feminist publishing collective.'

Sixteen

I am not impressed. 'It is not that kind of memoir.'

'What do you mean?'

'I am not a man-hater.'

'Neither am I.'

'It is a serious memoir,' I tell her. 'I will find a proper publisher for it.'

'Good luck,' says Gwendolyn quietly.

'I danced with Diaghilev,' I tell her severely. 'I will have no trouble finding a publisher.'

'Maybe they'd be interested if you'd written a book about Diaghilev,' Gwendolyn murmurs, her nose practically in her chicken Kiev.

'I have had a very interesting life,' I say. 'Once they read my memoir, they will buy it at once.'

❈ ❈ ❈

I have lunch with a man I know in publishing. We talk for three hours and drink a lot of wine and he is charming to me. I tell him about my book. He is very excited.

'There is a big market for ballet books,' he says.

I begin to tell him what the book is about. His interest cools noticeably.

'I thought you meant something for children,' he says. 'Something with pictures. There's always a market for those. If it was something like that I'd be interested. But I can't see that there's a market for your life story unless you're really famous.'

I tell him that my life story is very interesting and that I have met many famous people. I mention Diaghilev. He has not heard of Diaghilev.

But I am not put off. He was not the right publisher, that is all. There are others, and if my book cannot be published here then I will send it to England, where they have a true appreciation of ballet. I will certainly find a publisher there.

❋ ❋ ❋

I write to the person who edited that lying, offensive, idiotic know-nothing biography of Teddy. (Who is Sylvia Sampson-Harris anyway? She certainly never came and spoke to me. Her book is not a real biography. It has no footnotes, no references. A factual book should have footnotes and references. It is obvious to me that she just sat down with Teddy and listened to his stories. Does she not know Teddy is a fantasist and a liar? The whole thing makes me sick. It is a tissue of lies, and it does not even mention Teddy's baroque private life. How did it ever get into print?) I tell the editor I have written my own memoirs which are *at least* as interesting as Teddy's. I tell him I wish to set the record straight on certain matters regarding Teddy's history with my ballet company. I offer to send him the manuscript. A substantial length of time elapses. I receive a letter. It says:

Dear Mrs Black,

Thank you for your letter. As a general rule we do not publish memoirs unless the subject has a sufficiently high public profile to generate sales. Our decision to publish the biography of Edward Larwood was based on his international fame as a performer. While I am sure your own career is not without interest, your name does not have the same recognition factor as his.

Sixteen

While I cannot offer you any hope of publication, I wish you well in your endeavours and thank you for your interest in our company.

I do not write any more letters after that.

❋ ❋ ❋

It is my birthday. John thinks I am turning sixty-seven but in fact I am turning seventy-two. Hurrah.

Gwendolyn and the children come to lunch. Gwendolyn has bought me a scarf (hand-made by one of those artsy-craftsy women she's friendly with these days, but it's not so unattractive, considering). Simon has bought me some handkerchiefs. Sophie has bought me a cartoonish picture of a ballerina with eyes as big as Bambi, mounted on card and surrounded with a frill of lace. It has a hook on the back. It is to go on my wall, she says. It is a hideous object but the thought is charming.

While we are eating lunch (asparagus quiche, my new specialty, with home-made bread and an avocado salad, and lemon cheesecake to follow) I discover that John and Gwendolyn have conspired to give me one more present. It is a book, bound in white leather, with marbled pages and gold lettering on the cover.

'What is this?' I say.

'Read it,' says John gleefully.

It says: *My Life in Dance: the memoirs of Galina Koslova.*

'We had it privately printed,' says John.

'I typed up the manuscript,' Gwendolyn adds.

'Does it have any pictures?' asks Sophie, reaching for it.

'We had fifty copies made so you can give some to your friends,' says John. 'I hope that was all right,' he adds anxiously.

I have tears in my eyes.

'Thank you,' I say, and hug John. He was always the sweetest, kindest, most considerate of men.

It is a beautiful object. I can scarcely believe it. They have done a very good job, very professional. You would never know it was not produced by a real publisher. I leaf through it. I am struck by how different the words look on the page, printed rather than hand-written, so confident, so solid. It is almost as if they were written by someone else. Strangely, I feel that the memoir is no longer mine. Gwendolyn has typed it and strangers have laid it out and printed it. There can be no more elaboration or explanation. People will read it and make of it what they will. If they misunderstand what I have written, I cannot be there to set them straight. My memoir has taken on a life of its own.

Seventeen

Posy walked into Teddy's office.

'I think you should see this,' she said.

'What is it?'

Posy handed it over. It was a book, expensively bound in white leather, with gold lettering on the cover. *My Life in Dance*.

'One of Galina's friends showed it to me. It's the talk of the town, apparently.'

Eighteen

An invitation arrives. Another fundraising dinner. Artists of Ballet South will appear, it says.

'Shall I tell them we're not going?' John says.

'On the contrary,' I say, 'I would love to go.'

'Why the change of heart?'

'Because now everything is different. Everyone knows.'

'Everyone knows what?'

'The truth.'

'About?'

'Him.'

John looks alarmed. 'What are you talking about, Galina?'

'They have all read my memoir. Now that they know the truth, they will certainly get rid of him.'

'But why would they do that?' John is staring at me as if I have gone completely insane.

'Isn't it obvious? He does not deserve this company. He will ruin it. They must get rid of him.'

'Darling, nobody's going to cancel his contract because of your memoir,' John says.

'Why not?'

'Because it just doesn't work like that. He's doing a good job. Everybody's very happy with him. Maybe he's learnt from his mistakes.'

'Didn't you *read* my memoir?' I snap. 'He is incapable of learning from his mistakes. He is a monstrous egotist. He does not create, he can only destroy.'

'Darling, this has got to stop,' John says. He is becoming impatient. 'I know you've taken a set against him but, to be honest with you, I've got no idea why. And yes, I *have* read your memoir but I don't really understand why you blame him so much. He probably shouldn't have quit when he did, but the thing had pretty much run its course. You were barely hanging in there as it was.'

'What do you mean?' I say.

'The company would have gone under anyway,' John says. 'It wasn't viable.'

'It was!'

'It wasn't, Galina. You were barely making ends meet. It was a nice try but the time wasn't right. It was never going to work.'

'Did you think this at the time?'

'You know I did.'

'No, I do not think you ever said this to me before.'

I feel betrayed. He was my backer. He was my *business partner*. And yet he did not have faith in me. I wonder about

Eighteen

the company's swift demise and whether perhaps we could have found ways to keep going. Perhaps, perhaps. Too late now.

'It was all a long time ago,' John says soothingly. 'I know you're still upset about it, but it's time to let go of it, it really is. "We all lived happily ever after", remember?'

He smiles encouragingly at me and after a moment I smile back. I am angry at him but there is no point making a scene. We both know he is not the one I am really angry with.

❊ ❊ ❊

'Galina,' cries Elaine, 'what a surprise!'

They all turn to look at me — Elaine, Valerie, Phillipa — and I wonder whether it was such a good idea to have distributed my memoir among my friends. The gala crowd is out in their glad rags for the Ballet South fund-raiser. I have bought a new dress for the occasion and do not look half bad for an old girl.

'You're the last person we expected to see,' Valerie says, giving me one of her insinuating looks.

'I always try to come along to these little dos when I can,' I say with dignity.

'You've missed the last few,' Valerie points out.

'So have you seen him yet?' asks Phillipa.

'Who?'

'Teddy,' they chorus.

I scan the room casually. 'No. Is he here yet?'

'I heard he's read your book,' Valerie says, watching eagerly for my reaction.

'Really?' I say smoothly, as if I couldn't care less.

Of course I am hoping that he has read my book. I have come here to confront him. I do not know what I will say yet but I am sure something will come to me when I am face to face with him once again. John has warned me not to make a scene, but I don't care. This is my moment and I will not let good manners rob me of it. My stomach is full of butterflies and I realise I have stage fright. I have not felt this way in many years and yet it seems strangely appropriate. A return to the old me. A tray of champagne comes past and I grab one and toss it down. My hand with its many rings looks like a claw. Not quite the old me then.

Some sixth sense prompts me to look around. There is an eddying by the door, a little susurration of excitement.

It's him.

I have seen his picture in the paper and seen his mug upon the television so I thought I knew what to expect, but in the flesh he still surprises, for he looks uncannily the same. Yes, his hair is white, his knees arthritic, he no longer moves with the elasticity of a dancer, but his face, still strangely smooth, is the face I knew in 1946. He looks like he has made a pact with the devil. He scans the room and our eyes meet. He starts; I know he has seen me, but he is on public display now, there is no time to talk.

We are summoned into the dining room before I can get to him. Pale prawns are served, drowning in an ocean of seafood sauce, followed by a pale rubbery substance, possibly chicken, in a sweet apricot puddle. Teddy stands up and makes a speech. It is about new and innovative choreography. I have heard this speech before and I do not listen to the details. I tune in again when the applause begins. Teddy steps down from the podium

Eighteen

and the lights go down. A dancer appears at one end of the parquetry dance floor in a spotlight, dressed in the costume of a faun, and the insinuating curve of a flute plays the opening notes of *Prélude à l'après-midi d'un faune*. It is a surprising choice for a charity bash — I was expecting the *grand pas de deux* from *Nutcracker* or *Sleeping Beauty* — something crowd-pleasing, anyway, not a horned and half-naked man sliding insolently onto the dance floor as if he has just peeled himself out of an Arcadian fantasy. But this was always Teddy's signature piece so I suppose I should not be surprised that he has revived it. I wait for the three girls to appear, lured by the faun, as they do in every other version of the piece I have ever seen, but there are no girls in this one, only another boy in Grecian attire, a boy as exotic and alluring as the first. I watch in astonishment as boy and faun, faun and boy, play together in a sinuously beautiful duet, scandalous and sensuous as a dream. I wonder where Teddy found them, for Alice McDowell never had boys like this (milksops all, poor things). But these boys, these men, are gods: powerfully physical, wonderfully sensual, skilful, sensitive, and yet masculine. I watch them dance together and, as the spell creeps over me, a new idea appears in my mind. All of a sudden I know what went wrong between me and Teddy all those years ago. I know what his secret was.

I am floored. I am devastated. I am sickened and stunned and mystified and a million other things in a dizzying rush. Should I have known? Did everyone else know? Was I a fool? I thought I knew everything about my dancers; I made it my business to know. I thought I was a good judge of character. But I did not know this.

Too soon the piece is over — ten minutes gone in the twinkling of an eye — and the audience is clapping uncertainly and whispering and rustling and trying to work out if they just saw what they think they saw, but they don't dare to ask in case they're wrong, and I glimpse Teddy congratulating his dancers (who have miraculously turned from gods back into puppies) and I can see the smile on his face, his look of mischief and delight, but he is nervous too. I know that tinge of uncertainty around the mouth. I wonder if it's me he's worried about.

'What was that thing about anyway?' Valerie's husband asks. 'Looked a bit sus to me.'

'It is Greek,' I explain. 'Like the illustrations on vases.'

'The unspeakable vice, eh?' someone murmurs, and they all snuffle merrily.

Dessert arrives (a terrine, pink-flavoured) and a mood of fat contentment descends over the table, any lingering disquiet soothed away by large quantities of sugar. The confection sickens me and I give it to John, who has a sweet tooth. After the dessert is cleared away, a big band appears and starts tooting and blatting their way through 'Hello Dolly'.

'Can we go home?' I ask John. 'I do not feel well.'

'There's someone here I've got to talk to,' John says. 'I'll just be a few minutes.'

John disappears to talk business with some other tuxedoed men. I look around for Teddy but he is nowhere to be seen. The temperature in the room begins to rise as the gala crowd shake a leg. The room is blue with cigarette smoke and I move out onto the terrace, hoping for some fresh air and quiet. It is a

Eighteen

miraculous Adelaide night, still and hot, the air as dry as parchment. But it is quiet out here and the night air is soothing after the smother of the air-conditioning.

'Hello, Galina.'

He is standing at the other end of the terrace, smoking a cigarette; I see the tip glow and then fade in the darkness. There is half a moon in the sky and it shimmers off his white head.

'I was hoping we'd have a chance to speak.'

'I have nothing to say to you.'

'I read your memoir.' His cigarette glows again. 'You don't have a very good opinion of me, do you?'

'Who cares what I think?'

'You'd be surprised. I've been getting some pretty funny looks around the corridors of power.'

He is smiling. He thinks this is a *joke*.

'I am thinking of writing a new chapter,' I say. 'There is a lot I left out.'

'Yes, I noticed,' he says, smirking.

'I was not in full possession of the *facts* when I wrote my memoir,' I shout. 'I did not know that you were a *pervert* and a *sodomite*.'

'Galina, please —'

'You *trifled* with me. I gave you a job, I gave you a chance. How could you treat me like that?'

Teddy's bantering smile is still frozen on his face. He has nothing to say to me. His eyes are terrified.

'Was it all just a game to you? Did you think it was funny?'

'No!'

'Then why?'

John appears. I know he has heard me shouting. 'There you are, darling,' he booms. 'I've been looking for you everywhere.'

'John, this has nothing to do with you,' I say.

'Somebody was asking for you, Larwood,' John says. 'Better not neglect your guests.'

Teddy looks grateful for the interruption.

'Excuse me,' he says. He flicks his cigarette away into the darkness and squeezes past me to disappear inside.

'Coward!' I scream after him.

He does not look back.

❄ ❄ ❄

'I warned you not to make a scene,' John growls as he marches me towards the car.

'He is a coward,' I say. 'He is despicable.'

'What was all that about, anyway?'

But I cannot tell him.

Nineteen

It was hard not to be a little in love with Teddy. When he first joined my company he went out of his way to make himself agreeable to me. Naturally he was grateful to me for giving him an opportunity, and it seemed to me innocent enough: he would offer me little compliments on my appearance, the fragrance I was wearing, my *très chic* hat. Occasionally he would bring flowers for no reason. At company rehearsals, whenever I looked at him I seemed to find him looking at me, and he would give me a secret smile. He would appear on my doorstep in the evenings with champagne and a new gramophone record, or a book, or some poetry, and I would invite him in and give him supper and we would talk and talk and talk.

I had not met anyone like Teddy before and did not understand his modus operandi. For a while, I even believed that he was in love with me. But then I realised I had it the wrong way round. It was not that he was in love with me, he wanted *me* to be in love with *him*. It was not enough that he should be admired for his work and cheered by audiences. He had to feel that everyone he came in contact with loved and adored him, but as soon as he had conquered them his interest would wane and he would turn his attention to someone new. For him, the seduction was the thing, the challenge of winning hearts and minds, the pure artistry. The women he chose were generally older than himself, clever women who amused him and were not over-awed by him: a dressmaker I had found to design our costumes, who had spent some time at an atelier in Paris before the war; a balletomane with a rich husband who took to slumming with Teddy for awhile, before he lost interest in her and dropped her. Sophisticated women, no longer in the ripe and idiotic flush of youth, who liked his clever talk and the smooth flow of his compliments, but were not so gauche as to expect undying love or a marriage proposal. He wanted our love but would give nothing back himself — nothing, that is, that might cost him something. He lived for the adoration of others but, like the stage performer he was, he preferred to keep his admirers on the other side of the fourth wall.

A ballet company is always a hotbed of romantic entanglements. It is inevitable, when you put so many young people at such close quarters, that there will be romantic feelings from time to time. After Teddy had been with the company for about a year, one of my girls, Agnes, started walking out with Derek, one of the boys. They were very much in love and it was rumoured that they would soon be getting

Nineteen

engaged. But then, for reasons known only to himself, Teddy began to pay Agnes certain attentions which were very familiar to me: he gave her compliments, bought her gifts, took her out for intimate suppers. All of this attention soon turned Agnes's head and she began arriving at company class on Teddy's arm, acting very proud and snubbing poor Derek, who was quite broken-hearted. Although it was not generally my practice to interfere in the private lives of my dancers, I felt compelled to take Agnes aside. 'Derek truly loves you,' I warned her. 'I would think very carefully before throwing that love away on a whim.' Naturally she did not listen to me.

A week or so later, Agnes and Teddy swanned into class together half an hour late. Neither were in practice clothes and Agnes was sporting a diamond engagement ring. Teddy strutted around letting the other dancers congratulate him, utterly disrupting my class, while Agnes gave me a look of triumph. Derek had to be taken outside and given a glass of water. They announced that they would be married in the spring and everyone was invited to the wedding.

For those in the company who, like me, had assumed that Teddy was an incorrigible bachelor, this sudden decision came as a great shock.

'What do you suppose he's up to?' Posy asked, when Teddy and Agnes had made their exit.

'I have no idea,' I replied.

'I wouldn't have thought she was exactly his type,' Posy said.

I couldn't have agreed more. Agnes, though a sweet girl, was fifteen years Teddy's junior and, with the best will in the world, she was no match for him. The two of them together were like

Red Riding Hood and the Wolf. I could not imagine what Teddy was thinking, and I feared for her.

The engagement lasted less than two weeks. Before Agnes had even chosen a dress pattern, Teddy arrived on her parents' doorstep and told her the wedding was off: he had changed his mind and he could not marry her. Agnes collapsed and did not come out of her bedroom for two weeks. I heard, although I don't know if it's true, that before Teddy left he asked for the engagement ring back.

'Why did you do it?' I asked Teddy. 'Why break that girl's heart?'

'I didn't set out to do it,' Teddy said. 'It just happened.'

'Why ask her to marry you if you didn't intend to go through with it?'

'I did mean it at the time,' he insisted. 'I just got cold feet.'

He could never bear to admit responsibility for anything.

❉ ❉ ❉

We started rehearsing *The Snow Queen* in the spring of 1948. We had been dancing together for two years and I thought I was immune to his charms. When he started coming round to my house again, paying his little attentions, did I rebuff him? Laugh at him? Send him away with a flea in his ear? No; I did none of those things. I let him in and I enjoyed his company. I should have been warier. I can see that now. But I believed that I was safe from him. Not just because I knew him, his tricks and his ways, but because of who I was.

I always prided myself on my discipline. I believed it was the

Nineteen

one thing that had made me successful in life. I could master disinclination. I could master physical exhaustion. I could dance with a fever, with an injury, without sleep; in short, I could work in any situation, no matter how extreme or uncongenial, if I chose to do so. I thought I was the mistress of my own body. It was not until we began to rehearse *The Snow Queen* that I discovered I was not.

When two people have danced together for a long time, an intimacy develops that goes beyond words. Those of us who are fluent in the language of the body can say much more with it than we could ever manage with our stupid and unskilled tongues. Our skin, our eyes, the touch of our hands, the angle of a shoulder, the turn of a head, speak a language of muscle and sinew, chemical and blood, which is unmistakable and, because it has nothing to do with our conscious minds, it does not lie.

As Teddy and I rehearsed *The Snow Queen*, something began to happen which had never happened before. I do not know where it came from. There was no obvious trigger. One day there was nothing between us, the next day there was *something*. Shards of magic mirror lodged in the human heart? I cannot explain it. But as we moved deeper into the new ballet, an attraction began to grow between us which was quite involuntary and quite unstoppable. At first I could not allow myself to believe it. I am imagining it, I thought. It cannot be. But I knew it with every fibre of my being. I could feel it taking hold. We were being drawn swiftly into deep water. It was quite inexorable. This was nothing like our little flirtation in the early days. That had been a matter of the ego, but this was something of the body and it was soon entirely out of my control.

I could no longer dance coolly and professionally if Teddy was in the room. The matter-of-factness which makes lifts and *pas de deux* possible had deserted me. Every touch of his hand upon mine sent me into a reeling spin. It was like having a temperature or being drunk. It was out of my control and I could do nothing about it. I could say nothing to Teddy and I could say nothing to Posy. I did my best and I managed not to fall. But my confusion and dismay were intense.

Looking back now, I wonder what I was thinking. Did no alarm bells ring? Did I heed no warnings? What was the matter with me? But the truth was, I was in love. I had never been in love before. I was utterly unprepared for that derangement of the senses and I fell, head over heels, I fell. This was like nothing I had experienced before. The first time it had been a flirtation, nothing more. This was something else and, what was more, I sensed and felt and knew in my bones *that he felt something too*.

In spite of everything that happened afterwards, in spite of everything I now know, I still believe this to be true. This was not wishful thinking. For a moment, for a brief moment, I *know* he loved me.

And what did I think the night Teddy came to my bed? Did I think I had found my one true love? That we would now be together for ever? That this was *happily ever after*?

I thought all of these things, and nothing at all. As soon as I opened the door to him that night, I suspended all my critical faculties. I knew it was going to happen before it happened,

Nineteen

and I wanted it so much I never stopped to think about what might happen afterwards.

He ran a mile, of course. That's what happened afterwards. I knew he had run away when he went missing. I knew it was not really about his failed ballet. He fled because he could not face me.

❈ ❈ ❈

In her memoirs, Mathilde Kschessinska recalls going to see the great Marius Petipa, then the *maître de ballet* of the Imperial Theatres, and asking him to revive the ballet *Esmeralda* for her. Virginia Zucchi had had a great success in this role and Kschessinska wished to tackle it herself.

Petipa asked her, 'You love?' (His Russian was always poor.)

Kschessinska replied that yes, she was in love.

'You suffer?' he asked next.

Kschessinska, who was then very young, replied, 'Of course not!'

Petipa then explained to her that only an artist who had known the sufferings of love could understand and interpret the role of Esmeralda. Kschessinska was not at all impressed by this reply, but later, when she had indeed known the sufferings of love, she discovered he had been absolutely right.

I heard this story from Kschessinska herself when I was a young dancer at the Imperial Ballet School, and I was just as sceptical as she had been. I could not see what love or suffering had to do with being an artist. Surely being an artist was about technique? I did not realise then that while feeling without technique is little more than hysteria, technique without feeling is merely geometry. At its best, ballet represents the union of the mind and the spirit, the head and the heart, technique and emotion. When the emotions are frozen (or, let us say, undeveloped), technique, no matter how perfect, runs the risk of becoming robotic.

Diaghilev often accused me of being a robot. 'You are as cold as ice!' he would scream at me. 'You look as if you are dead inside!' He was often cruel to his dancers. To him, we were little more than pawns moving about the stage, doing his bidding. He was a great man, but he was not a nice man. I did everything I could to please him, but it was never enough. I worked hard — much harder than anyone else — and I had tremendous stamina. They sometimes called me Stalina — woman of steel — because I would keep working even when everyone else was exhausted. And what a dancer I was! My line was exquisite. My limbs were very long and my movements were liquid and silky smooth. I had the highest extensions of anyone in the company, I never lost my balance in a pirouette, my thirty-two *fouettés* were as solid as a rock. I was a wonder — everyone said so — but I never rose beyond the position of senior soloist. I never graduated to principal. I was given leads sometimes in the most modern of ballets, the plotless ones which were about purity of expression. I was cast as the Spirit of Progress, or the Machine Age. I was the Twentieth Century, I was a Muse. I was once the Statue of Liberty. But I was never cast as Aurora or Odette or Giselle. The parts I had dreamed of all my life never came to me.

I could not understand why. I worked and worked and worked. I worked until my feet bled and I could not hold my

Nineteen

arms up for tiredness. I made myself into the most perfect dancer I could possibly be. But still it was not enough.

I went to Diaghilev. I said, 'What must I do to become a principal?'

And he said, 'You must first join the human race.'

Twenty

1948

'You'd better come quickly.' Deirdre's voice on the phone was flat. 'Mother's in hospital.'

A stroke. It had come without warning: one minute she was doing the breakfast dishes, the next she was slumped on the floor, her legs crumpled under her, dishwater from her gloved hands soaking her skirt. Deirdre had found her at lunchtime, insensible. She'd been there all morning, soapsuds turning to scum in the sink.

He stood at the foot of her hospital bed, gazing down at her. She looked small in the bed, pale, her hair lifeless and flat upon the pillow. It felt slightly indecent to see her lying there in a flimsy nightgown, his mother who never ventured out without many layers of cloth between herself and the world, his mother who was always fully dressed, even at the breakfast table. Now here she was, as defenceless and downy as a baby bird tucked up in a nest, fast asleep in a deep, deep sleep. Comatose. And would she wake up again? The doctors said they didn't know.

He could not decide what to make of it. Mother, in hospital, perhaps brain-damaged, close to death. She was still young — he was not sure how young exactly, but probably not yet sixty. Already a widow, of course — Father had been carried off by a heart attack at fifty-two. (He had been away then, overseas. The telegram had not found him — he had been on tour — and by the time he received it, Father was already in the ground.) Father's death had not hit him hard, but this, this was something else altogether. Looking down at Mother in the bed — the thin chest rising and falling — he knew himself to be quite calm, but at the same time he felt as if he had been in some calamitous accident, had had a leg or an arm torn off, but the shock was preventing the signals from reaching his brain; the realisation had not quite hit him yet. But soon enough he knew the shock would wear off, and he would start to scream.

❈ ❈ ❈

He spent the afternoon on his own, drinking whisky and listening to smoky jazz fresh off the boat from America. At tea time there was a knock on the door. Teddy's heart jumped with surprise and pleasure when he opened it to Archie, one of the boys from the company. Archie was as toothsome as ever, blond-haired and beaming, as wholesome as cornflakes and milk.

Twenty

'This is an unexpected pleasure,' he said, noting with dismay how slurred his voice was. He was drunker than he'd realised. 'Come in.'

Archie didn't seem to notice, bouncing down the hall with a spring in his step.

'What are you in such a good mood about?' he asked.

'I've got some news,' said Archie, almost bursting out of his skin with excitement.

'Well?' Teddy poured him a drink, which Archie accepted absent-mindedly.

'I'm getting married!' Archie blurted, beaming.

Teddy stared at him, feeling his skin contract. A rush of blood went up his face and he hoped it wasn't as visible as it felt.

'Married?'

'I proposed to Yvonne and she said yes. I was rather hoping,' he added coyly, 'that you'd be my best man.'

'Me?'

He knew he sounded like an idiot. He struggled to get a grip on himself.

'Of course, my dear,' he said, 'I'd be honoured. Thrilled. When's the happy day?'

'We thought sometime in the new year, after the tour's over.'

'Excellent,' Teddy said faintly.

For a moment they stared at each other.

'You haven't congratulated me,' Archie said, a tiny frown appearing between his pale golden brows.

'Haven't I? How rude of me. Congratulations. I'm sure you'll both be very happy together.'

Archie grinned at him and then he grasped Teddy's hand in both of his and pumped it enthusiastically. 'I reckon I must be just about the happiest man alive,' he said.

'It certainly looks that way,' said Teddy. 'Let's have another drink.'

And after all, what had he expected? He had always known Archie the handsome chorus boy was going out with Yvonne the pretty little coryphée. Their romance had been the talk of the company and everyone thought it was *simply adorable*. It was only a matter of time before they had a wedding and became a golden couple and she started producing little golden children. It was the way of the world.

❊ ❊ ❊

The whisky was finished and Archie had gone home some time ago.

I will go for a walk, Teddy thought, with a fearful and licentious prickle of the skin at the back of his neck, and with that aim in mind he put on his plainest mackintosh and pulled a hat down low over his face and set out. It was a still desert night, the sky clear and black, sharp-starred, the air refrigerated. The streets were quiet in this early-retiring town and he listened to the lonely sound of his heels cracking sharply with each footfall on the wide empty pavements. He turned right, then left, and began to head down towards the river through an avenue of plane trees, listening to the leaves above him rustle and sigh. As he walked down the gentle slope the temperature began to sink and a dank chill started to seep through his mackintosh into his clothes. The air thickened, becoming moist, condensing into mist

Twenty

as he found the path that ran along beside the river. A duck quacked sleepily and he heard something rustling in the reeds — a rat? — but saw nothing.

He slowed, tensing, as he heard the sound of footsteps approaching, but when the figure emerged from the trees he saw it was only a dog-walker. The man went plunging past, neck sunk into his collar, bristling hostility. The dog, a Maltese terrier, sniffed at Teddy curiously but did not stop. It occurred to him a dog would make a convenient prop in this sort of situation. All innocent and above board — just taking the dog for a walk. Although he wasn't sure what you'd do with the dog if ... Not that he made a habit of this sort of thing. Or liked dogs.

His eyes were adjusting to the moonlight now and he began to walk more slowly as he passed through the trees. The air was filled with the tiny sounds of a river at night — splashes and plops, flappings and patterings — and further away he could hear a lion grumbling behind the high walls of the zoo. The tall gums stood thin and straight like sentinels among the bushy bulk of the scrubby melaleucas. The ground crackled with fallen seed pods, fallen bark, kindling to start a royal blaze, and he could hear the shift and crunch of feet he could not yet see moving over the littered ground. Then the tall shapes of the trees began to resolve themselves into other shapes, smaller shapes, and men began to appear, silent as ghosts in the darkness, wary, watching, waiting. Heads turned in his direction, heads with hats pulled low, faceless. The unseen eyes scrutinised him and he stared back, then selected someone almost at random, a young man by the look of him, still in his army coat, and began to move towards him. The young man allowed him to approach and then turned, moving deeper into the screen of scrub, letting Teddy follow. When they could no longer be seen from the path, the younger man stopped and turned to face him. With slow deliberate movements he began to undo the buttons of his coat. Underneath, Teddy could see that the young man's fly was already open and he shivered, hit by a thrilling mixture of revulsion and desire. Suddenly he felt very drunk, thick-tongued and clumsy. The young man stared at him impassively. Teddy dropped to his knees.

Suddenly there was a crash and the foliage began to thrash and heave. Somebody went hurtling past them in the dark and the silence of the night was fractured by torchlight and the ear-piercing screech of a policeman's whistle. The young man took off, crashing away with heavy boots through the trees, and Teddy staggered to his feet, filled with terror. All around him men were stumbling and lunging. Bobbing torchlight seemed to come from every direction. It was an ambush. Teddy began to run. Close, too close, men were being handcuffed, thrashing like netted fish, growling and swearing. A policeman's face leered suddenly in the beam of a torch. There was an almighty splash as someone plunged into the water — by accident or design, who could tell? The torches began to converge on the river's edge and Teddy went tearing off as fast as he could in the opposite direction, careering through the trees, slipping and tripping, hoping to God he didn't stumble over a tree root and break his ankle. He ran and ran, and gradually the torchlight and whistles and the clank of handcuffs receded into the night, and he realised that there would be no heavy hand of the law falling upon his shoulder tonight. He exploded out of the park

Twenty

and onto the road, and began to walk briskly home, his heart hammering out of all proportion to the physical exertion of his run, reminding himself to walk slowly — a man running, alone at night, would only look suspicious — but he did not relax again until he was safely inside his own door once again, and that door was safely locked and bolted.

❊ ❊ ❊

'It was worry that brought her to this, you know,' Deirdre said, giving him the same narrow look she gave her kids when she suspected them of raiding the biscuit tin.

'What do you mean?'

'She thinks you ought to find some nice girl and settle down. She's worried you're going to end up alone.'

'Are you saying this is all my fault?'

'I'm not saying it's your fault,' Deirdre said, 'I'm just saying she had a lot of worries.'

'About me.'

'Yes.'

'And that's what made her have a stroke.'

'Yes.'

'Is that what the doctors say?'

'They're not saying anything much,' Deirdre sniffed, 'but I know Mum. It was worry that brought her to this.'

'It's a stroke,' Teddy said irritably. 'They're caused by blood clots. She doesn't have brain fever, you know.'

'You never considered her,' Deirdre accused. 'You don't spend any time with her, you don't go to see her —'

'That's not true!'

'You don't care if she worries herself sick about you.'

'She didn't worry about me!'

'Well, of course she wouldn't tell you how she really felt,' Deirdre said smugly. 'She wouldn't want to upset you. But she was worried about you.' She gave him a narrow, accusing look, a blackmailer's look. 'She thought it wasn't normal. A man your age, still not married.'

'She said that?'

'Yes, she did.' She knew she'd rattled him and her little eyes glinted with satisfaction. 'She thinks it's time you settled down. Started acting your age. Found yourself a wife.'

'Just like that?'

'You meet girls all the time in your line of work. They can't all be too fussy.'

She gave him a malicious smile. That was his sister: mean right down to the bone. But then she'd always been like that. Deirdre and Teddy had hated each other instinctively from birth.

❅ ❅ ❅

He was never popular when he was young. He was too skinny and weird-looking. Kids are ferocious, and instinctive, like feral dogs. The neighbourhood kids had pinned him as different before he even knew it himself. He could never work out how or why, but once the taint was identified it was indelible.

Mother was the only one who never teased or mocked or threw things at him, never let him know with uneasy glances and disappointed looks that he was not up to scratch, that he was alien and lacking and wrong. Mother loved to dance and sing. It was Mother who first took him to see a musical comedy, and

Twenty

didn't laugh when he danced all the way home. ('I'll take a strop to you, boy!' Father said when he saw him 'carrying on', as he put it. He couldn't blame the old boy, really. Father couldn't imagine getting through life as a sissy. He was only trying to help.) Mother enrolled him in dance classes, made him costumes, let him go on the stage. It was Mother who found a place, the only place, where her protean boy could be everything he wanted to be, where his wayward tendencies would be celebrated, not stifled. She loved him, she truly loved him, and she never tried to turn him into an ordinary little boy, never, never. To her, he was precious, and she never wanted to see his special lustre dimmed.

He had never been popular; had never really been liked. But the first time he stepped on a stage, everything changed. The proscenium arch was like a window onto another world where a different set of rules and standards applied. In the theatre no one minded if you were showing off; no one expected you to live down to the monosyllabic, brutish, thuggish, senseless standards of a teenage boy; no one called you names or mocked your feebleness at sport or your over-emphatic hand gestures or your neat clothes or your close friendships with frilly little neighbourhood girls. When you were on a stage you were free from all that, but, most miraculous of all, *so were the audience*. In a pantomime or a ballet or a performance of Shakespeare, ordinary people who lived by the most repellently narrow-minded standards would come to spend a little time in a place where they could feel, and dream, and suspend judgement for a while, and experience delight, before going back to the drudgery of their hellish suburban lives. It was the only place they would ever allow themselves to love him.

❄ ❄ ❄

Galina slapped a picture book down on the table.

'I think we should make this into ballet.'

Posy reached for the book and turned to the page Galina had marked. Teddy leaned over curiously. The story was called 'The Snow Queen'.

'Very dinky-di,' he remarked.

'What?' Galina gave him a steely look. She never did understand when she was being teased. He saw Posy smirk.

'Not much snow in Australia,' he explained.

'Why does that matter?'

'It doesn't,' he sighed, and lit a cigarette.

'I have rearranged the story,' Galina said. 'Not so many characters. Here I have notes. I also have the music.'

She handed Posy some handwritten notes and a record. Posy just nodded, neutral, turning the record over and studying the sleeve.

'I will dance the Snow Queen,' Galina said. 'Teddy will be Kay. I thought Yvonne for Gerda.'

In spite of himself, Teddy flinched. Galina didn't notice.

'Unless you wish to dance Gerda yourself.'

'I'd rather not,' Posy said. 'Can't take rehearsal and dance at the same time.'

'I would like to begin rehearsals in one week,' Galina said. 'Can you be ready?'

Although Teddy was gasping at the outrageousness of the request, Posy didn't turn a hair. 'I think so,' she said.

'Good. Then I will book rehearsal room.' Galina turned to him. 'And you, you will be ready to start on Monday?'

Twenty

'I hadn't given it much thought actually.'

'I will need your cast list by Friday.'

'How am I supposed to know how many people I'm going to need until I know what I'm doing?'

'You must decide,' Galina said. 'Quickly.'

❋ ❋ ❋

He only had himself to blame for this one. He had done a number on her — a new kind of ballet, a ballet that reflects new realities, a truly Australian ballet for a new generation, blah blah blah. At the time he even intended to do it, had all kinds of pie-in-the-sky ideas about what he could do, but she had capitulated a little too readily and now, unexpectedly, he had to come up with the goods.

'We will do double bill,' she announced, sounding like she was announcing a five-year plan. Or a purge. 'We will tour.'

It was his big chance. He knew he couldn't afford to mess it up. But recent events had overtaken him and he wasn't ready to start a new ballet. Not even close. What was he going to do?

❋ ❋ ❋

'It's such a sad story,' Posy said thoughtfully.

'But they all live happily ever after.'

'The Snow Queen doesn't.'

'But she's the villain.'

'No she isn't.'

'Then who is?'

Posy put her head on one side. 'You are.'

'Typical,' Teddy said lightly.

'But didn't you notice what a strange story it is? It's full of women who live alone and are desperate for company.'

'And they solve their problems by kidnapping young men.'

'Or young women.'

'That's not sad, that's sick.'

'It's very sad,' Posy said, looking at him seriously, and Teddy felt his colour rise.

'I've never really thought about it before,' Posy continued, 'but she must be very lonely.'

'Who? Galina?'

'She doesn't have a boyfriend or a husband —'

'She'd eat a boyfriend for breakfast,' Teddy chortled.

'But think about it. She's a long way from home, her English isn't very good. Apart from Andrei there's no one she can speak Russian to. She must be very lonely.'

Galina's fairy tale book lay open on the coffee table and Teddy looked down at the illustration, which showed an impossibly tall and thin Snow Queen in a triangular white robe like a frozen Christmas tree, a foot-high crown of ice towering upon her head. She had witchy black eyes and pointed fairy ears and, in the picture, the village boy gazed up at her with the big round eyes of a child. Something moved in him and he laughed uncomfortably, suddenly unsure of himself.

'She probably has a secret life,' he said. 'Armies of rent boys who arrive in the middle of the night. All very discreet of course, cash up front, no questions asked.'

Posy looked perplexed. 'What's a rent boy?' she asked.

❆ ❆ ❆

Twenty

Although he was not usually very attentive about that sort of thing, for some reason he knew it was Galina's birthday. He did not, of course, know how old she was, since, like every other dancer he had ever met, she lied about her age. At first he thought about letting the occasion slide (he was pretty ambivalent about his own birthdays), but some impulse landed him on her doorstep in the cool blue evening with a bunch of daffodils.

'Happy birthday,' he said, brandishing them as she opened the door.

She was obviously not expecting visitors, for she was wearing a plain house dress and no make-up. He had almost never seen her like this before. Even at the theatre, she arrived fully made up and then disappeared into her dressing room to take off one face and put on another. There was something disturbingly naked about her face; the eyes, usually so black and commanding, looked pale and tired. She looked at him, and looked at the flowers, and her face seemed to slump. She sneezed explosively and then burst into tears.

'Galina,' he said alarmed, 'whatever is the matter?'

She gulped something out and he discerned 'allergic' amongst it.

'Easily fixed,' he said and tossed the daffodils into the gutter. 'Now come on. Come and sit down and tell me what's wrong.'

Ignoring her resistance, he barged in the front door and manhandled her down the hall, into the sitting room and onto the settee. He tried to put his arm around her, but she pushed him violently away, so he knelt on the floor at her feet and waited as she cried and cried. When the sobs had subsided to an occasional sodden hiccup, he took her hands in his.

'Now what's this about?' he said. 'I'm sure it's nothing we can't sort out.'

'How,' she gasped, 'did you know it was my birthday?'

'I know all sorts of things about you,' he said.

She looked at him fiercely for a moment and blew her nose.

'I doubt that very much,' she said.

'I hate birthdays too, if you want to know the truth,' Teddy said. 'That's what happens when you set your heart on being an *enfant terrible*.'

She barked out a short laugh and blew her nose again.

'Thirty was dreadful. Thirty-four was worse. I'm about to hit thirty-six shortly and I'm not looking forward to it at all. You're not to breathe a word of this to anyone. The kids in the company think I'm thirty-one — at the very most.'

'What does it mean anyway?' she replied, with a flicker of her usual bravado. 'A birthday. It's just a number.'

'Exactly. Just a number.' He tried to peek under the curtain of black hair dangling limply about her face, but she wouldn't let him. 'Go on. I've told you my awful secret. What's yours?'

'A lady never discloses her age.'

'You've been at the Jane Austen again, haven't you?' But he didn't push. He had a fair idea.

'Pavlova danced until she was fifty,' Galina said. 'So did Kschessinska.'

So that was what was bothering her.

'Things were different then,' she said. 'It is not so long ago either.'

'Have you thought about what you'll do when you retire?'

Twenty

Her lip trembled, but she gazed off into the distance until her spilling eyes cleared, and then replied, bleakly, 'How can I retire?'

'You don't plan to die in the saddle like Pavlova, do you?'

'If I could, I would be very happy.'

'But you've got the school. You can always go on teaching.'

'Teaching?' she spat. 'You have never tried it.'

'Well no, I haven't —'

'I hate teaching. It is all frustration. Most of the girls are no good. They will never be any good. They do not work, they are lazy, they don't care. About dancing! To me dancing is everything, but they just don't care! Sometimes I want to throw them all out, every single one of them; I want to scream at them and say, come back when you can be serious, or never come back at all. Why do you come here if you are not prepared to work? But this I cannot say. They are my pupils and on them my livelihood depends, so I must teach them as if I hadn't noticed them slacking off and talking and giggling. It drives me wild! And occasionally I do find a girl with some talent. I try to encourage her, I try to do whatever I can for her. But these girls are like jellyfish, they are so weak and spineless. When I correct them, they cry or they sulk. I try to make them understand it is for their own good, but they do not understand and so they give up and go away. The good ones slip through my fingers and the bad ones waste my time. I did not become a dancer to live in a classroom. The classroom is the means to the end and the end is to be on the stage. The stage is everything, everything. You know this. Every day, I am just waiting to be onstage again, to be beautiful, to be alive. This is what I love, this is what I live for. But I always wanted to be the best. This was always my intention, and for this I worked hard, harder than anyone. But a time comes when to work is not enough. My back is too tight, my feet are too sore, my neck is too stiff. If I have given a long program, sometimes I am so broken I cannot sleep with the pain of it. And then the next day I must get up and do it all again, and I am so tired I can hardly bear it, but what am I to do? Who am I if I do not perform? I am no one. I am nothing.'

She stopped as abruptly as she had started, and for a long moment Teddy stared into her haunted eyes. He knew that sense of vertigo. The terror. *What am I, if I am not this?* He felt a sudden dizzying rush of tenderness towards her — this woman with her sparrow bones and the ruined feet he could see poking out of a pair of embroidered Chinese slippers — as if all the muscles and fibres that held him together had turned all at once to golden syrup. It was visceral and real, this feeling, but it was not lust — he was familiar with those chemical surges, in all their transcendent variety. It was something else, something rich and magnificent and pure. Something like love.

'It's knees with me,' he said. 'I hurt the left one when I was at Sadler's Wells. It got better, but they warned me if I hurt it again I might have to have an operation — I might not even dance again. Then I hurt the right one. I'm on borrowed time now.'

'I had noticed this. You are careful about them.' She looked down at him. He was kneeling on the floor. 'Perhaps you should not sit like that.'

Twenty

He unfolded himself slowly and slung himself into a chair. His joints were throbbing.

'And what will you do,' she asked, 'when they break down?'

'I don't know,' he said truthfully. 'I've thought about a few things. Maybe I could still choreograph.'

'You will not make a living,' she said.

'Let me hold on to the dream a little longer,' he protested, laughing.

'What is the point?' she said sombrely. 'You must be realistic.'

'Not without a few more glasses of gin in me,' he said. 'On the subject of which, you wouldn't happen to have a little splash of something about the house, would you?'

But she didn't. Galina was too spartan in her habits to have alcohol in the house.

'But it's your birthday,' he said, riskily. 'Aren't you going to celebrate with a little something?'

'I was not planning to celebrate at all,' she said, raising a pencil-thin brow, 'until you forced it on me.'

What is happening here? he wondered. In the two years he had known her, he had never seen her let down her guard like this. Oh, he had spent hours in her sitting room, yacking away about art and life. But that had been work, like having afternoon tea with the headmistress — sit up straight, mind your manners, no straying off the subject. Galina would give him the benefit of her experience, argue with him, disagree with him, order him about and put him in his place, but she would never veer into anything dangerously personal. He knew a lot about her career, about her training, about The Way Things

Were Done In The Imperial Ballet. But he had never glimpsed anything that might resemble a feeling. Now, suddenly, it was like she was unravelling before his eyes.

'Well, if you don't have gin perhaps I could make do with tea. You must have tea.'

She rose gracefully from the couch and went into the tiny kitchen. The bench held only a samovar and a tea caddy and he watched while she made tea and sliced lemons. The room had a tenuous, unused air; she knew how to make one or two simple dishes but, as far as he could see, she lived on cigarettes and toast.

'Is this the only thing you brought with you from Russia?' he asked, gesturing towards the samovar.

'That is from Sydney,' Galina said. 'I have nothing from Russia.'

'What, *nothing*? Nothing at all?'

'I left everything in Paris. I thought I would be going back for it. I don't know what happened to it.'

'You don't even have photographs of your family?'

'No.'

She handed him a cup of tea and headed back into the sitting room. He was stunned by her toughness. He carted a whole suitcase full of sentimental objects with him wherever he went: lucky charms, his favourite tea cup, the cardboard crown he'd worn as Prince Valiant when he was twelve, a nest of photographs (Mother, Pavlova, the cat he'd had when he was a little boy). He could not imagine venturing away without them.

'You cannot,' she said, as he sat down again, 'get too attached to *things*. They are too easily lost.'

'And what about people?'

Twenty

'What do you mean?' she asked warily.

'Have you ever been too attached to anyone?'

'Are you asking me if I've ever been in love?'

She looked at him curiously. There was a new note in her voice, as if he had unwittingly said the magic words and opened up the door to Ali Baba's cave.

'I suppose I am.'

'I would not be human if I had not.'

What a strange answer, he thought. 'So what happened?'

'It did not work out,' she said.

'Why not?'

'He did not feel the same way.'

He felt his scalp prickle. 'Who was he?'

She looked up suddenly and her large dark eyes met his, serious and disturbing. 'No one you know.'

Oh, I think I do, he thought, and his heart started to bang insistently against his chest.

'I have company to run,' Galina said, turning her face away and sipping her tea with studied casualness. 'I have no time for love.'

'But how can you live like that?' The thought of such a barren life filled him with horror.

'What choice is there?' she murmured.

'There's always a choice!' he said, his own simmering panic making him sound angrier than he was. 'You've got to *try*. You can't just let things slip away. This man, you should have —'

'What?' She turned on him, a flush rising to her cheeks. 'Thrown myself at his feet? Begged him to love me? The answer was no. Why humiliate myself?'

'How do you know what the answer was? Did you ask him?'

Her face blazed. 'I did not have to.'

'I bet if you went and found him right now, if you said to him "Johnny, I love you," and kissed him —'

They were staring at each other, eyes locked. She was frozen in place, a glass of tea trembling in her hand. Her wrists were like twigs.

'And if I did,' she said, 'what do you think would happen?'

'Something quite extraordinary.'

Her bright eyes studied him and he felt as if there wasn't enough oxygen in the room. Tantalising possibility crept in on subtle velvet feet and his skin prickled with a shiver of expectation.

'What a pity he is on the other side of the world,' she said, and the mood of enchantment collapsed. 'More tea.'

She disappeared into the kitchen.

Teddy did not follow her. He knew a tactical retreat when he saw one.

❈ ❈ ❈

Posy never made another ballet as beautiful as *The Snow Queen*. It began with the music: Debussy, weird and inward, the music of the unconscious, creeping and insidious, left-handed and strange. It was alchemical: the story and the music and Posy's exquisite choreography and Teddy and Galina all combined to create something as fragile and fantastic, as coldly beautiful as snow. It was a glimpse through a magic mirror into the dark side of the human heart, the heart poisoned with loss and longing, frostbitten through isolation, absence and exile.

Twenty

Teddy and Galina and Yvonne and the company (Archie danced the reindeer in *papier-mâché* antlers) assembled every morning in the rehearsal room and Posy would act as a lightning rod for the passions and tensions locked up in those hearts. Something began to hum in that bare, dusty space, something sinister and mysterious, as Posy marked out entrances and exits, allegros and adagios, solos, *pas de deux*, happy peasant dances, whirling snowflake dances. Every day the room would heat up until it was like an oven and the sweat would stream from the dancers' bodies, but beyond the heat and humidity lay a colder, chillier place, a palace of ice, where a spirit was trapped for eternity and young love simmered and bubbled away, heedless and selfish.

Whether by accident or design, Posy's rehearsal schedule had left Galina's two big set pieces — a *pas de deux* and a solo — until last. It was raining the day that they rehearsed the solo for the first time, and the company had not been called for the rehearsal. The three of them were alone in the hall and the rain was so loud upon the tin roof that it was difficult to hear the music. But Galina could hear it, even when it wasn't playing; it was as if it was already under her skin, a part of her, part of her blood, and she could hear its insistent throb in her own pulse-beats. Posy and Galina had always been closely attuned, but on that day there was something uncanny taking place, almost as if they were communicating without words. Teddy sat on the floor and watched them both, Galina so gaunt in her habitual black, Posy, round and red-haired, in tights and a red and white polka-dot top, as young and innocent as Minnie Mouse, moving like twins, almost like lovers, mirroring one another. Posy would begin to move and Galina would follow, sensing the movement before it was completed, two arms, two heads, moving in a dance of desolation and sorrow, the outpourings of a frozen heart liquefied at last by grief. The choreography was subtle and beautiful — not technically demanding, but deeply moving because of the quality of the emotion embedded within it.

Teddy had never seen Galina dance like that before, not ever, and as he watched her he was transported back into the past: 1929, his birthday treat (he was seventeen). The night he first saw Pavlova. She was old then, and less than two years away from death, but she had a quality which went beyond technique, beyond words. There were plenty of ballerinas who were more technically accomplished, but none with her charisma, her passion and her soul. Most of her repertoire was rubbish — even she admitted that — but when she danced, the choreography no longer seemed to matter. She was a great artist and she could invest almost anything with such feeling that she transcended the material and turned it into gold.

Galina, on the other hand, was usually as precise and perfect as a mathematical equation. Her line was flawless. She danced with the icy precision of an angel wielding a sword of light. Her technique was invulnerable — there was no possibility that she could fail or fall. Her flawlessness was her flaw. But that day he saw the cracks in the carapace, a tiny glimpse of the soul which she kept hidden away. There in the rehearsal room, with only Teddy and Posy as an audience, Galina gave the greatest performance of her life.

It took them two hours to make the solo, only two hours, with no false starts and hesitations, no backsliding or forgetting

Twenty

what came next. It unfurled like a bolt of silk, as if the solo had already existed in both Galina and Posy's minds and had only been waiting for them to discover it and reveal it and fix it in memory for ever. Two hours, and they were like women in a trance, barely speaking, communicating in half-sentences, like mind-readers, and at the end of it all, when the rain had finally ceased on the roof and Galina had danced it from beginning to end, the two of them stood in the studio, exhausted, wordless, staring at each other. Posy finally broke the silence.

'That'll work,' she said.

❋ ❋ ❋

He was supposed to be taking a rehearsal for his own ballet that afternoon, but instead he went and sat by his mother's bedside. She seemed small and shrivelled, a mannequin, not quite life-size. She had not yet woken from her deep slumber. Days had passed without the slightest change. She wore a different floral nightgown today — Deirdre had been busy washing and ironing enough nightgowns to dress an army — but she was otherwise perfectly unchanged. It was eerie. She should be in a glass case, Teddy thought. Or a castle surrounded by a forest of thorns and sleeping courtiers.

'Did I ever tell you about the time I was touring with *Aurora's Wedding*?' he asked into the silence. Mother's chest rose and fell unchanged, but he told himself she was listening. 'We were touring England with a program of *divertissements* and *Aurora's Wedding* was one of them — it's the last act of *The Sleeping Beauty*, the one with the Bluebirds and Puss in Boots and all the fairy variations.

Anyway, we were in some dreadful place, I can't remember where, and we'd been called for company rehearsal. It was winter, and bitterly cold outside, and all the windows in the rehearsal room were closed. We had only been working for a few minutes before one of the girls fell down in a faint, and another started to swoon. Everyone started to panic, but then someone opened a window, the two girls revived and so the rehearsal continued. But then, when they let us go for lunch, someone closed all the windows again because it was freezing outside. I had an errand to do, so I went out for about half an hour, and as soon as I came back I knew something was wrong. A theatre with a full company in it is never quiet but that day it was totally silent, so I went to the dressing room to see where everyone was. The room was filled with girls and they were all fast asleep. Some of them had fallen asleep at their dressing tables, lights blazing, mugs of tea cooling, cigarettes burning to ash. Others had keeled over where they stood. It was as if they were all enchanted, I've never seen anything like it. I tried to wake some of them up but I couldn't, so I ran to tell the stage manager, and along the way I found more company members slumped on the floor like discarded dolls. It turned out the boiler had been leaking coke fumes into the rehearsal room and they'd been spreading into the rooms around it. Everyone woke up again once we opened a few windows, but a few of the girls had to be taken off to hospital. Aurora's wedding was very sparsely attended that night.'

His mother's face was smooth and impassive, so blank it seemed hardly a face at all.

Twenty

'You would have liked it if I'd married, wouldn't you Mother?' he said. 'S'pose it's a bit late for that now.'

❊ ❊ ❊

He drank too much that night, although he hadn't intended to get drunk, and it was with the greatest difficulty that he stopped himself ringing Archie, although he wasn't sure what he wanted to say to him. Eventually he lapsed into a distressing and dream-ridden sleep populated by phantom versions of Archie and Galina and his mother, screeching and beseeching by turns, drawing him close and then pushing him away. He found himself once again face to face with Archie, screaming at him this time, pouring out his hurt and his disappointment and his rage in a torrent of abuse, while Archie, polite, mild-mannered Archie, turned into the kind of spitting, cursing, hate-filled boy he remembered from his childhood — and then Mother was there, weeping, with a terrible reproachful look on her face, and he realised she'd overheard his argument with Archie, *she knew* — and then, after a confused jumble of panic and fear about getting to a railway station on time, he was on a sleeper train with Galina, and in the dream he knew it was the Trans-Siberian Express, and the walls were red plush and the carriage was rocking with a sly and insistent motion and Galina was watching him with a sly and insistent look and then in a plushy crimsony haze the two of them were engulfed by an erotic dreaming fug, coupling as the train rocked on, kathunkathunk, kathunkathunk —

He woke up sticky, hungover and startled. He ran a bath, smoked a cigarette, then smoked another. It didn't help. He brewed himself a coffee in the Turkish style and sieved the dregs of it through his teeth. It cut through the fuzziness of his hangover but did nothing to clarify his thoughts. The mood of the dream was sticking so resolutely to him that he felt as if he was moving through toffee; an erotic residue clung to everything, dogging his thoughts, slowing his mind, and not even the prosaic reality of his nasty bathroom and even nastier kitchen could drag him back into the everyday.

He set off for rehearsal in a state of barely suppressed excitement. His stomach was shimmying as if he was about to go onstage, but he did not examine the feeling too closely.

Posy was humming to herself when he arrived, marking out movements as she waited. Galina was standing in a plume of smoke like a dragon, but stubbed out her cigarette viciously when she saw him walk in.

'You're late,' she snapped. 'And you stink. You should not drink when you have rehearsal.'

The real Galina could not have been less like the Galina of his dreams if she tried, and for a moment his mood of erotic expectation faltered, so that he almost laughed at himself. But as they worked their way, haltingly this time, with many pauses and recapitulations, into the *pas de deux* in which the Snow Queen seduces Kay, something began to creep into the room, a mood, a flavour, a strange aroma that made his skin tickle and his pupils dilate. They had danced a hundred love duets together — every *pas de deux* is about love — but never one like this. Once Galina's eyes locked onto his they would not let him go, and they circled one another, testing, feinting, feeling each other out, fighting, flirting, annihilating each other with the intensity

Twenty

and intimacy of their gaze. Sweat poured off him — pure alcohol, he suspected — but she was as cool as ice. Her skin under his hands was slippery as a dolphin's, but his grasp was sure; he would not let her fall. Time after time, Posy forced them together then ripped them apart, until he was almost ready to scream with frustration. But at last, finally, she brought them together in one climactic surge — Galina flew up into the air, high above his head, floating weightless on his one hand — and then gravity claimed her, she spiralled magnificently into his arms, and the *pas de deux* was over. The last strains of the music died away but he didn't release her, and she didn't pull away. For a long moment they stood there, staring into each other's eyes. He could feel her heart hammering through her skin, hammering against his chest. Her eyes, black, looked fathomlessly into his. And he knew exactly what she was thinking.

❋ ❋ ❋

Later, he told himself it was the alcohol that did it. He had brought the very best champagne he could find — champagne was something he knew about — when he turned up on her doorstep the night of the *pas de deux*. He told himself he was there to celebrate a successful day, there was nothing more to it than that. Two friends having a glass of champagne. Nothing untoward about that. True, she didn't drink much of it — 'How can I drink when tomorrow is rehearsal?' — but she had a glass, and a glass was enough. Music was playing, jazz, smoky and decadent (did she like that sort of thing, Galina, the champion of Petipa and Tchaikovsky?) and before the bubbly had even begun to flow he could feel that galvanising atmosphere, that weird enchantment creeping over him once again. What am I doing here? he asked himself, watching her eyes follow him around the room. He wanted to laugh. The atmosphere in the room was so charged he felt twice as alive as usual. I can't do this, it's impossible. But it seemed like nothing more than a piece of delicious wickedness to think about breaking that essential rule: do not sleep with the boss. Why not? Why the hell not? Some madness was upon him, and he liked it. She was dangerous and she was forbidden for a hundred thousand very good reasons and so he knocked back a glass of champagne and then he knocked back another and then he took her wrist tightly in his grasp, and drew her towards him, and kissed her. Her skin was so soft, so smooth it was like kissing air — a phantom — but then she began to kiss him back and soon there was no stopping them.

❄ ❄ ❄

He could not quite imagine sleeping beside her in her bed, waking up, having breakfast together. It seemed altogether too intimate. So once a suitable interval had elapsed, he got up, dressed and made his way home.

It was two in the morning and there were no taxis to be seen anywhere, but he didn't care. He felt exhilarated. A wonderful, a marvellous solution was unfolding before his eyes, an answer to all his problems, and all Galina's problems too.

They would get married!

He found he was giggling as he walked along the street. Tomorrow he would go to the hospital straight away. Mother, he would say, Mother, I've found someone. If anything could

Twenty

bring her out of her coma, it was news like that. Assuming the shock didn't kill her. I've found someone. She's only ten years older than me. She's a dancer. She's my boss. She's a White Russian who danced for Diaghilev. She's got a horrible temper and she's a chain-smoker. You're going to love her.

He could see Mother frowning slightly as she struggled to come to terms with his astonishing news. 'And why do you want to marry this woman?' she asked.

'Why not?' he replied. 'We have a lot in common. We both love ballet. And she adores me.'

'But do you adore her?'

He could see her looking at him with those mild, faded-blue eyes, so soft and yet so intelligent, and he could not quite meet her gaze.

'I admire her,' he said. 'And I like her. Although I find her a little bit frightening, to tell you the truth.'

'That doesn't sound like a very good basis for a marriage.'

'But we're a good match. We work well together, we're complementary. And if we were married we'd never have to worry about being lonely.'

'It would be wrong to trick this woman into marriage because you're afraid of being alone,' Mother said gently.

'I wouldn't be tricking her into anything,' he protested. 'Don't you see? It's the perfect solution for both of us.'

'It doesn't sound like a very good idea to me, darling,' Mother said. 'I do hope you'll give it some more thought.'

But can't you see I'm doing this for you? he cried, silently, as the vision faded and he found himself walking alone down dark, windy streets. The air smelt of wattle and it was very cold. His exhilaration had quite faded, but still he clung to his idea. He was going to marry Galina and they would both live happily ever after. He was sure of it.

❈ ❈ ❈

Rehearsal the next morning would be the test. How would she behave towards him? Would she be flirtatious, tremulous, shy? Resentful? Dismissive? Furious? He arrived at rehearsal on time for once — it seemed best not to do anything too provocative. She was quiet when he arrived — Posy was already there — and preoccupied, but otherwise she was admirably restrained.

'Good morning,' she said, nodding to him.

'Good morning,' he replied.

She was a cool one all right.

Rehearsal proceeded smoothly, calmly, with none of the dramatic tension of the last few days. They went through their paces like horses in an elaborate dressage, all angles and placement, brisk and businesslike. Posy made corrections and adjustments, the music tinkled over and over, the sweat ran from their bodies and spattered the dusty floor with round brown splots. It was a day for mechanics, not artistry, and the morning soon sped by.

'Would you like to have lunch with me?' Teddy asked Galina, as she towelled herself off at the end of the rehearsal. She had been so remote all morning, he still had not the slightest idea what she was thinking. He was wondering whether or not to float the marriage idea. He hoped that once they were alone he could get a better sense of her state of mind.

Twenty

'That will not be possible,' she said, in her grating voice, 'I already have lunch engagement.'

'Oh.'

'Perhaps another time then?'

'Yes. Another time.'

He wondered how to read her answer as she disappeared into the changing room. Did she really have another lunch engagement? Was she playing games with him? Or was she simply trying to avoid him because she was mortified by what they had done? She didn't *seem* mortified. But then how could you tell?

She was a long time getting changed, and when she appeared again she was wearing a very smart suit and some fanciful shoes.

'Who's the lucky fellow?' Teddy asked, feeling a weird flicker of jealousy.

'It is business,' Galina said tersely, as she pulled on her gloves. 'By the way, I need report from you on your new ballet. You will give to me tomorrow.'

His heart started skittering anxiously. 'It's not ready yet.'

'Designer needs time to work. You will tell me tomorrow how work is proceeding.'

'I don't think I can be ready tomorrow.'

'You will tell me tomorrow.'

She turned and walked smartly out, her heels hammering on the hollow wooden floor. He watched her go, filled with a dreadful uncertainty. Was this going to be his punishment? Was she about to take his ballet away from him? But how had she known it wasn't ready? Did she have a spy in his rehearsal room? But no — he was being ridiculous. The deadline was short and she had a company to run. She was entirely within her rights to ask him how it was going. But still, the timing was alarming.

Posy was looking at him curiously. 'How's it going anyway?'

Normally he could confide in Posy. But not about this; not now. 'Fine,' he lied.

❊ ❊ ❊

If it hadn't been for Mother, he told himself, it all would have been fine. He would have come up with a scenario and found some great music and made something truly exciting. He'd had so many good ideas — or at least bits of ideas. If he'd just had the chance to really focus, he knew he could have made something really great out of them. But he didn't have a starting point, he didn't have a scenario. He didn't have anything, and whenever he tried to begin, his thoughts scattered and frayed. He could not concentrate; it was impossible to keep his mind off that little figure in the hospital bed, and his spoiled career, and the hopeless wreckage of his life. He wished he was the kind of choreographer who could just take a fairy tale and knock something together (not mentioning any names). But he was not that kind of choreographer — he would have been embarrassed to do something so old-fashioned. He had standards, ideals. He had become a choreographer because he wanted to say things, about himself, about his people, about his country — even if it was just to berate them for their anti-intellectualism, their complacency, their dull narrow-minded conservatism, their lack of passion. He had so many things he wanted to say! If he could just work out how to get started ...

Twenty

❈ ❈ ❈

'I have the most amazing news.'

Posy. She was practically jumping up and down with excitement on the other end of the phone.

'You know John Black?'

'Mr Washing Machine?'

'He's asked Galina to marry him!'

It hit him with the force of a blow. His throat closed convulsively.

'And what did she say?' His voice came out sounding strangled.

'She's giving him an answer tomorrow. I say, isn't she a dark horse! And here was I, worrying that she might be lonely!'

Posy burbled on, but Teddy didn't hear any more. Another day, another engagement. First Archie and now Galina.

'Everyone in the world is getting married,' he said faintly.

'Except us,' said Posy. 'What do you think? Maybe you and I should make a go of it.'

'Ha.'

'I wonder if she'll ask me to be a bridesmaid?'

He cancelled his rehearsal and went to the art gallery, hoping to find some inspiration for his stalled ballet. He gazed at the Madonna-blue skies and blistering sunlight of the Australian Impressionists and almost had something for a moment — something about light and air, something almost abstract — but his mind soon wandered to Galina, and whatever he'd had was lost.

John has asked her to marry him. Of course she's going to say yes. Why wouldn't she?

As he sat in the almost-empty art gallery, listening to the soft echoing footfalls and staring unseeing at the large light canvases, he was filled with a queasy sensation that was a little like seasickness, as if he was bobbing up and down on a greasy and turgid sea of unfamiliar emotions with no land in sight. He was filled with terror, a visceral, primal kind of terror, as if the world had suddenly decided to stop making sense, leaving him stranded in a demented realm which bore only a passing resemblance to the one he was familiar with. But the problem, he realised, did not lie with the world. It was in himself.

He had seduced Galina. (He could see that now. He'd been moving towards her for days, weeks even, before the night of the *pas de deux*, circling her, ensnaring her.) He had wanted to marry her. But then, when he was almost at the brink, John Black had snatched her away from him. And what did he feel?

Relief.

Dismay, jealousy, fury. But also relief.

Thoughts surged around his head, clashing and colliding. *But I love her. I want to marry her.* He had it all planned. They would build a life together, a life in dance, working together, dancing together. It would be a full life, a useful life, a satisfying life. And she loved him. God, how she loved him, with all the pent-up force of a woman who poured her life into her art. Imagine all that energy directed at him! Surely, surely that would be enough to carry them both through any doubts and uncertainties? If I marry Galina, he thought, I won't feel that itch any more, I won't need to go out into the night, looking for —

Whatever it was that he looked for.

Twenty

I've been waiting, he thought, for the right girl, and she *is* the right girl, I know she is. Because if it's not her, then it's not anyone.

But she is marrying John Black.

And why shouldn't she, after all? If he was honest, if he was truly honest, he knew he could not offer her the kind of love and devotion John Black was offering (not to mention the material wealth and the big house and the ready-made family ...). Mr Washing Machine was solid and reliable and unambiguous. No uncertainties, no doubts, no hidden corners, no secrets. When a man like that fell in love, there could be no doubt that he meant it. Whereas Teddy —

Did not love her as she deserved to be loved. A suffocating sense of failure crowded in upon him. Somewhere amid the steaming jungle of his thoughts was an awareness that there was something in him, some vital spark which was always pulling him in another direction, and, however much he tried to ignore it, it would always be there.

But I love her.

Not enough.

What he wanted most of all was the chance to escape from ambiguity, to be simply and straightforwardly *in love*. She had seemed to offer him a way into that quiet life that other people enjoyed, a way of living blamelessly, openly, without the many layers of deceit and defeat and disappointment, being able to give love its true name without fear or shame. He wished that someone could wave a magic wand and make him in love with Galina. Everything would be so simple if he could just be in love with Galina.

But he didn't love her, not like that. He admired her, he even desired her; but not in the same way that he'd desired Archie, that desperate, gnawing, panting, rend-the-flesh-from-his-bones kind of desire. He had wanted to crawl inside Archie's skin and dwell there, poor, polite, idiotic, conventional Archie.

But so what? Couldn't he marry Galina anyway? And if from time to time he had a private adventure — well, she wasn't to know, and what she didn't know couldn't hurt her, could it? He had known men who lived like that, married men, *known* them, oh yes, known them and found them despicable. But then some people could hold a lot of contradictions and a lot of dishonesty in their lives and never feel a thing.

But he had missed his chance. Which had never really been a chance anyway. Galina was going to marry John Black.

He was astonished at how disappointed he felt. It was savage and bitter, as if all along he'd been keeping one last card up his sleeve, his get-out-of-jail-free card, only to discover when he tried to play it that the card was blank and he was trapped.

Marrying Galina would solve everything.

It would solve nothing.

It would make Mother so happy.

It would end in misery.

But she loves me.

But you don't love her.

I was happy in London, he thought. I had a life I loved there. And I threw it all away because I had to chase a boy who didn't want to be chased. (He hadn't told Galina the whole truth about that kid from the chorus and why Miss de Valois had dismissed him.) So here I am in a place I never wanted to be,

Twenty

living a life I didn't want to live, where I'm unhappy, and the career I've built for myself is in ruins because tomorrow Galina is going to take my ballet away from me and there are no second chances. I've thrown away every opportunity I've ever been given because I couldn't stop chasing boys long enough to concentrate on anything. I have ruined my life.

Footsteps shushed across the floor and he realised a uniformed man was standing in front of him.

'The gallery's about to close, sir,' the guard said.

To his horror, he realised that he had tears coursing down his cheeks. He stared at the brass buttons on the man's chest for a moment, then stood and moved dumbly towards the exit.

❋ ❋ ❋

He caught the train to Victor Harbor. They had gone there sometimes for family holidays when he was young and now it seemed like a plausible retreat. He wasn't sure what he hoped to find in this out-of-season temple of family fun, but when he arrived there he discovered it was weirdly comforting. It was a cold September and the place was deserted. The summer amusements were gone, the boarding houses all had vacancy signs swinging in the wind that howled off the Southern Ocean. All was wet, grey, windswept. He walked the beaches in silence. Seaweed was piled everywhere in huge black stinking mats, reeking of decay. Seagulls followed him in packs, eyeing him boldly, hoping for a sandwich crust or a chip. He had no idea what he was doing there or what he was going to do when he got back. His thoughts reeled and crashed with the surf, a ceaseless mucky churn, all grey water and sand.

He was there for four days. When he woke up on the fifth day it was time to return.

'Where have you been?' Deirdre screamed when he rang her. 'I've been ringing and ringing!'

Mother was dead. She passed away, as Deirdre put it, the day after he went to Victor. He had made it back just in time for the funeral. He wished he'd sensed that she was gone, but he hadn't. Immersed in his own private crisis, he'd felt nothing. Now it was too late.

❄ ❄ ❄

He stood at the wake among the aunties and uncles, the cousins, the friends, the neighbours, watching as they scoffed down lamingtons and ham sandwiches, jam tarts, sponge cake and cups of weak stewed tea, stuffing their faces while the world fell apart.

'At least I was there at the end,' Deirdre said, dabbing her eyes with a hankie, assuming a saintly air.

He wanted to kill her. He wanted to kill them all.

Blind with rage, he stalked out of the house.

Twenty-one

I am not angry at Teddy because he is or was or might be a homosexual. What I cannot forgive is his carelessness, the cavalier way he takes things up as if they were created for his own amusement and then throws them away again as soon as he is bored with them. The way he squanders things — the way he squanders *people* as if they are things — burning through us all as if we are nothing at all, because when you are beautiful and talented and charming like Teddy there is always someone else to take our place. Everything comes to him so easily! The rest of us must work and slave and aspire and fail, and for him everything is effortless. But because it all comes so easily, none of it means anything to him.

What could not I have done, given half his gifts? What could not I have accomplished? I gave my life to ballet, I worked hard for over fifty years, and at the end of it all, what have I got to show for it? Teddy was a dilettante and an egotist and a wrecker. He never worked as hard as I did. He never had it in him. Instead he flirted and dabbled and played, he flitted here and there, stealing love and devouring life, leaving chaos behind him, always so greedy for *more*, shying away from anything that seemed too much like hard work. In the Imperial Ballet School they taught us that if we wanted to be great we must work, and so I worked. Teddy never worked a day in his life.

And yet he is an artist. He is a great artist.

This is what I cannot forgive.

Twenty-two

The rest of the fund-raiser passed in a blur. He pressed the flesh, flirted and smiled, accompanied by the faint rustle of cheque books. He was bored and he was tired and his leg hurt and he wanted to be at home. More than that, he was sick at heart. *Sodomite. Pervert.* It wasn't the first time he'd been called those names, but it was the first time he'd been called them by Galina. What a way to meet, after all this time.

But what did you expect? he asked himself. You know she's got a grudge against you. She wouldn't have published that poisonous bloody memoir if she wasn't still pissed off at you.

Reading Galina's book had been exquisitely painful, like being stuck with red-hot pins. Her tortured locutions, her pronouncements about life and work and art, were so familiar to him that at times it was like she was there in the room with him. Time had reduced her to a caricature in his memory —

Galina in her dominatrix-of-the-classroom aspect, the stick pounding time on the floor, the rasping voice shouting instructions over the banal tinkle of a piano — but the memoir had brought back other memories. Her bare feet in a pair of Chinese slippers. The sense of unbearable longing she had brought to the Snow Queen's solo, so keen and wrenching it was almost impossible to watch. He looked back at himself, across a distance of twenty-five years, and it was like watching a train wreck in progress. He had been demented, out of control, the many uncertainties and insecurities of his life driving him at breakneck speed towards disaster. But even at the time, even as his wheels were jumping the tracks and the carriages full of screaming, yelping people were starting to collapse like concertinas, there had been a tiny part of himself that had known exactly what he was doing. He knew perfectly well how she felt about him. He had always known, of course he had. And when it all started to go wrong, and his life started falling apart, he had done the one thing he always did to make himself feel better. He had seduced her and he had made her love him. And then he had dropped her.

The band played their last number, the lights came up to full dazzle, and in the sudden hush the last of the gala crowd began to look around them and blink and search out handbags and jackets and keys and totter towards the car park. Teddy exchanged pleasantries with members of the board, the organisers of the dinner, a donor or two, and then stepped gratefully out into the summer night.

There was a cab waiting at the kerb but he decided to walk home. He did not have far to go and now he was out in the

Twenty-two

moonlight the ache in his leg no longer seemed so bad. The pavement was still radiant with heat from the day, but a soft wind had sprung up and he took off his jacket and tie and opened his collar so the breeze could ruffle the shirt on his back. It was one of the things he had always loved about this place, these summer nights, long and warm and dark. He remembered spending evenings with Galina, listening to music with the windows open wide to the night.

Nostalgia is a false god, he reminded himself. If things had ever been that way between them, they were not so now.

He tried to banish Galina from his thoughts by focusing on the success of the dinner and the stir he'd caused with his boys. How wicked they'd been, how decadent and bold! He'd have to send them something tomorrow, a thank-you card and a bottle of fizz. They'd certainly given the good burghers of Adelaide something to talk about over lunch, and wasn't that the real purpose of art? To enliven the dinner conversation?

I gave you a job, I gave you a chance. How could you treat me like that?

She would not be banished. An old woman in an expensive dress, her face gaunt, yellowed as parchment, every shadow like a bruise. But still a good hater. She'd always been a good hater.

Looking back it was always so easy to see how you could have behaved better, been kinder. But, at the time, there is never an opportunity for kindness because darker emotions are at work, fear and hatred, the primitive stuff, the stuff with claws. And somehow you find yourself biting and tearing and stealing and scratching and running, and it's only afterwards that you begin to think about what you should have done. I am capable of much greater kindness now, he thought. And then remembered how he had treated Cee at the end. Separating from him was like tearing himself away from a Siamese twin, protracted and bloody. And now he was alone — the one thing he had always feared. A taxi swooshed past and he wondered, too late, if he should flag it down, for his leg was hurting again. But the taxi turned the corner and disappeared before he had quite made up his mind to hail it, leaving him alone on the quiet street, so he had no choice but to keep on walking.

Had Cee been his last hurrah? At the time it hadn't seemed possible, but now he began to wonder whether the path ahead of him was a long descent into darkness, a descent he would make alone. He thought about beautiful Tony and the disastrous night of the gala, and the jaunty strains of some post-war jitterbug began clanging in his mind's ear. He could almost remember the choreography that went with that music, flashy and raucous and fun, the choreography of a ballet called *The Lodger*, in which youth and beauty mocked the humiliation of ageing desire. Time has its revenge on all of us, he thought. How Galina would laugh if she knew.

He tried to imagine that conversation. He could turn up on her doorstep carrying flowers and champagne, just like the old days. Would she invite him in or slam the door in his face? Probably the latter. And what would he say to her anyway? She had always been suspicious of words (although her English had improved out of sight since he first knew her — where had she picked up a word like *sodomite*?). Actions, for Galina, always spoke louder than words.

And what was it, then, that he wanted to say?

Twenty-two

Not *sorry*, exactly. Because he had done what he had to do, and she had done the same, and it had turned out badly, but then things often did. Not *you were right*, because she wasn't. She had the whole thing completely wrong and had never understood half of what he said to her, or did for her, she had misinterpreted everything. But, on the other hand, in one way she *was* right. The thing that they had made together, their company (and he did think of it as his, even if it had never had his name on it), had been precious and magnificent, for however short a time it had existed, and it had not deserved to be swept away by time. The company would never rise again; the company was dead. But he was still alive, and so was Galina, and so was Posy.

His leg was aching again. He had begun to suspect this nagging ache would not leave him now, it was the first of many tiny blows which, accumulating, would fell him in the end. But he kept on walking, for it was late, and there were no buses, no cars and no taxis in sight. The dark Adelaide streets were silent and empty under an old tarnished moon and his nostrils filled with the heady scent of eucalyptus. He walked slowly home, an old man with broken knees, and he thought about snow.

Twenty-three

Ballet South is mounting *The Snow Queen*.

I cannot believe it, but there it is in the newspaper in black and white. *The Snow Queen* by Posy Foster. They will be putting it on as part of their new season.

The article does not mention me.

❋ ❋ ❋

'Galina?'

'Yes?'

'It's Posy. Posy Foster.'

I have to sit down. I have been expecting and not expecting this phone call.

'I don't know if anyone at Ballet South's been in touch with you ...'

'They haven't.'

'Oh. Well, the thing is, we're mounting *The Snow Queen* and I was hoping you might be available to help coach the dancers.'

'Me?'

'I remember what you used to say about tradition. How important it was that things be handed down from one dancer to another. Living memory. I think there's a lot you could bring to the production.'

'My memory is not what it used to be,' I say, and wonder why I am playing hard to get.

I hear Posy hesitate. 'You do remember the ballet, don't you?'

'I am not senile yet,' I say.

Posy laughs. 'I'm glad to hear it. So are you interested?'

'I would be very happy to be involved, if you think it would be helpful.'

'Good,' says Posy.

'Why *The Snow Queen*?' I ask. 'Why isn't he doing one of his own?'

'I don't know. When Teddy asked me if I'd be willing to remount it, I didn't really want to look a gift-horse in the mouth, if you know what I mean. He did say he thought it was some of my best work.'

'The ballet wasn't even finished when he left the company.'

'Well, no.'

There is an awkward pause.

'I'll give you a call a bit closer to the time and we can work out what we're going to do,' Posy says. 'Perhaps we could have lunch?'

'Yes,' I say. 'I would like that.'

Twenty-three

❋ ❋ ❋

When I married John and moved into his house, everything I had collected during my years with the company came with me. There were boxes of papers, my few remaining costumes, all our correspondence, posters, programs, musical scores, design sketches. It all went into a shed at the bottom of the garden. When I was first married it was all too fresh and bitter, I could not bear to look at it; later, it did not seem to matter any more. I had a husband and a house to look after; we entertained frequently; I was busy. So it all sat in the shed, still in the original boxes, just as it had been packed, waiting for the moment when I would feel the need to look at it again.

I get off the phone to Posy and go down to the shed and turn on the light. We are lucky in Adelaide, where the climate is very dry, it is possible to store things for long periods of time without them becoming mouldy or musty. Insects are the only problem, insects and mice, and some of my cardboard boxes are chewed and feathery. But most are intact.

I find scrapbooks filled with newspaper clippings and turn over the stiff, yellow pages. How important it seemed, then, that this should be preserved! Reviews, articles, interviews. How proud I was of our achievement, what a pioneer I was. The first professional ballet company in Australia! I thought I was doing something lasting, something significant. Now it all seems meaningless — who cares what a motley group of dancers did twenty-five, thirty years ago?

I take my costumes from their wrappings. The whites have turned yellow and they are stained with wear, although I am sure they were cleaned before they were put away. I think it is age itself that marks them. The tulle has lost all its crispness — the tutus sag like wilting vegetables. Here I find tarnished gilding, there a bodice shedding beadwork as the stitching rots. At last I find what I am looking for: a long gown with a cape, white, trimmed with swansdown, the kind of thing Ginger Rogers might have worn. My Snow Queen costume. Something has feasted on it and it is honeycombed with holes. I long to put it on again (would it still fit me, I wonder?) but I know it would disintegrate. I find the crown which once accompanied it hidden in a shoebox. Like an old chandelier it has shed many of its crystals. I cannot bear to see such palpable evidence of decay and I fold them all away again in their mothball-smelling shrouds.

I collect some sketches and some scrapbooks, thinking Posy may be interested in them, switch out the light and lock the door, leaving my works once more to the silverfish.

❄ ❄ ❄

I have not been in a rehearsal room in more than twenty years. I do not own practice clothes any more, and the young people no longer wear the tunics which were fashionable in my day. To my surprise, I no longer have a pair of ballet shoes. I thought I might have kept a pair or two, hidden away somewhere in a drawer, but I must have been more ruthless than I recall when I gave away my old life. I put it all behind me with a vengeance, no mementoes, no relics. What I kept is locked in the shed. Everything else went to the tip.

But it does not matter because they will not expect me to dance. My role today is to advise, nothing more. Just as well,

Twenty-three

really: I could not bear to put on a pair of *pointe* shoes. My feet have been ruined by too many years of torment and they would not tolerate such brutal treatment now. This is the real reason Pavlova spent all those extra hours working alone: it takes that long to coax your stiffening body back into life in the morning, and to ease it into repose at night. I remember the feet that felt like a crunching bag of fishbones, the spine that locked up washboard-tight, the many muscles of the legs that had to be swished and stretched into motion, the blood-red filigree of a hundred little injuries. These are my daily companions now, now that I am in my seventies, now that I am old.

Rehearsals are being held in a beautiful old building in the city, a converted Adelaide bluestone with wide balconies and iron lacework. The studio is on an upper floor above a restaurant and the walk up the dusty wooden stairs sends my mind spinning back to other studios, other dusty stairs. How strange it is to be walking into rehearsal again. My nerves begin to fizz.

A door opens at the top of the stairs and Teddy appears, his long white hair rumpled like a cockatoo's crest. He sees me coming, stops and smiles uncertainly. And suddenly I know why I am here, I know why they are remounting *The Snow Queen*. It is his gift to me; an act of love; perhaps the only kind of love he is capable of giving. A shiver runs through me and I am helpless again beneath a flood of recollections, the torrent which has poured from me since the day I read in the paper that Edward Larwood was coming home at last: Natasha and Kschessinska, Diaghilev, the Koslova Ballet, Teddy and *The Lodger* and the fights and our last tour and the blow upon blow of the bad reviews and the shrinking houses and the half-hearted audiences and my best dancers, my precious children, slinking in one by one and telling me they were leaving to join Borovansky, or the chorus of a musical comedy, or the navy.

But then the years intervened and I put my past behind me. I retired. I listened to Gwendolyn reading and went to parent-teacher evenings and learned to play tennis and bridge. I bought and renovated and sold houses. I designed gardens and planned wardrobes and went on overseas holidays. I held soirées and functions and morning teas and suppers, went to many dos and dinners. I shopped like a rich man's wife, I cultivated my mind, I read the great works of English literature. Twenty-five years goes by in the twinkling of an eye. And I have been happy; yes, happy, more than I ever would have thought possible during my younger days, when I was contemplating retirement and wishing that, like Pavlova, I might just drop down dead between one tour and the next and never have to think about the future. And this, too, was Teddy's gift to me, for I know that if I had not broken the habit of a lifetime by falling so disastrously in love with Teddy, I could never have married John.

'I'm glad you could come,' he says warily, and I know he is expecting me to come after him with long knives and venom.

'I feel privileged to be here,' I say.

He smiles then and we both know it is going to be all right.

'Come upstairs,' he says, extending his hand to me. 'They're all waiting for you.'

We ascend the stairs together and emerge into a large light room with lofty ceilings and doors opening wide onto a

Twenty-three

balcony. The room is filled with the false perspective of mirrors reflecting and re-reflecting, the murmur of voices, a piano that echoes down the stairwell. As I enter the room, the voices stop and a cluster of young dancers turn to stare at me.

'*Madame*,' murmurs one, in the old style, and the dancers all perform an impromptu *révérence*. I find I have tears in my eyes.

'Hello, Galina,' says Posy, coming forward.

She is middle-aged and I am shocked. I know it has been twenty-five years but foolishly I was expecting the Posy I knew. She is still, I notice, covered in freckles. She introduces me to the girl and boy who will be dancing the roles of Kay and the Snow Queen. The girl is too young for the role, but all the dancers are young now.

'I've heard so much about you, it's such an honour to finally meet you,' the girl gushes.

I look at her sceptically and she explains, 'My mum went to your ballet school.'

'What was her name?'

'Elizabeth Green. You probably don't remember her —'

'Betty?'

'That's right!'

Betty. Extraordinary.

'I remember her,' I say. 'A promising dancer. She gave up too soon.'

'She always regretted it,' the young girl says. 'She encouraged me to stick with it.'

'It would seem it has paid off,' I reply graciously.

Posy takes the young couple through the *pas de deux*. I am surprised by how well trained they are and wonder if the girl is one of Posy's students. A strange feeling comes over me and I find myself wondering whether my company was not the most important thing I did after all. Perhaps the most important thing was my school. Choreographers die and companies collapse and dancers retire and memory fades, but even old dancers like me can still teach. The classroom is the beginning and the end of a dancer's life; the wheel turns and the future is spun out of the past. The girls I taught go on to teach other girls. It is there at the *barre*, among the five year olds who want to be ballerinas, that the real work is done, and it is there that my legacy persists. And, as I watch the dancers, I glimpse another life, a life I could have led if only I'd had more courage, a life of teaching and solitude, a life in art, the life Posy led, the life she is leading now. But I am not unhappy about the choices I made. Life is long and full of surprises.

I have not been able to listen to Debussy for a long time, but today I am unperturbed by it and I feel myself succumbing to the old enchantment, just as I did all those years ago. I look for an answering *frisson* in the dancers, but there is nothing to see. They are as perfectly formed as a pair of pole-vaulters, their technique pristine, but watching them, I cannot help feeling I am watching a circus act. Everything is planes and angles, balances and tricks. Their movements are beautiful and perfectly formed, but somehow — yes, I cannot avoid it — robotic.

I turn to Teddy and I know that he has been thinking exactly what I am thinking. He gets to his feet, with a dreadful elaboration of knees, and offers me his hand. Doubtful, I rise and the two of us move out into the middle of the studio floor.

Twenty-three

How grotesque we look, I think, as I glimpse our reflections in the unforgiving mirrors. My skin is fleshless and gaunt upon my bones. I look like death at the wedding feast. But Teddy is still Teddy — he cannot jump any more and lifts are quite out of the question, but his fine bold head is as magnificent as ever, his Roman profile only becoming more splendid with age and, as I take my position, I feel something beginning to surge within me and I no longer feel ridiculous. The music begins and we find our way carefully into the movement, feeling our way like blind lovers, walking where we cannot dance, and I am transported back in time to a moment twenty-five years ago when it seemed that my life, my hopes, everything I ever dreamed of, were hanging upon a knife's edge, and all my hopes of future happiness were tied up in this one man, who was just as frail and frightened and doubting and flawed as myself. Our eyes meet and I see him as he must have been then: ambitious and questing, thwarted, full of rage, rage at all that the world had to offer and all that the world had withheld. The rage of the perfectionist, always wanting more. We move together, through the dance of our lives, although age and gravity have tied us to the ground, and I experience once more, for the very last time, the visceral pleasure, which is more than just physical, of the life of the body.

And all too soon the dance is ended and Teddy is giving me his secret smile. Then he turns away from me and makes a joke about the lift which concludes the dance (it was acrobatic and spectacular, very daring in its day) and all the children laugh. And then he is gone — he has a meeting with the minister — and it is as if a light has gone out of the room. I return to my seat, my heart knocking in my chest, and Posy asks me to talk the dancers through the *pas de deux*.

'Try to imagine,' I tell them, although I am still struggling to catch my breath, 'that you are in the grip of a mad passion. You,' to the boy, 'have a splinter of poison in your heart that is making you crazy, and you,' to the girl, 'have a chunk of ice for a heart which is so cold that it burns you. You live in a frozen palace. You are a queen and you are immortal. You have been alone for thousands of years and you are desperate to find someone to love.'

The two of them nod at me wisely, but their faces are as blank as marionettes.

'Have you ever been in love?' I ask the dancers.

'Yes,' says the boy, and 'yes,' says the girl.

'Have you suffered?'

The two of them look at each other, embarrassed, and laugh.

'You will not understand these roles,' I tell them, 'until you have suffered for love.'

Of course I know that they don't believe me.

NOTE

Apart from the historical figures mentioned in passing in the text, all the characters in this novel are fictional.

References to the life of Mathilde Kschessinska are taken from *Dancing in Petersburg: The Memoirs of Kschessinska*, by H.S.H. The Princess Romanovsky-Krassinsky, translated by Arnold Haskell, London: Victor Gollancz, 1960.

The ballet *Terra Australis*, a version of which is attributed in the text to Teddy Larwood, was choreographed by Edouard Borovansky for the Borovansky Ballet in 1946. An account of the ballet appears in Edward H. Pask's *Ballet in Australia: The Second Act, 1940–1980*, Melbourne: Oxford University Press, 1982.